Of all the court  ry, how could she and same four walls? H welling up inside of her, Nancy came down hard on the sink with her fist, immediately regretting it when pain shot through her right hand from the assault. Grimacing and holding her throbbing hand to her breast, Nancy caught sight of her tearstained, flushed face in the mirror over the sink. Her eyes were red and swollen; she looked nothing like the woman she faced in her mirror this morning. That woman had still been glowing from a weekend of love and visions of a secure future. This woman into whose eyes she looked now was afraid of what the future might hold if Monica exposed her deception.

WHEN WE PRACTICE TO DECEIVE

GLORIA MALLETTE

An Original Holloway House Edition
HOLLOWAY HOUSE PUBLISHING COMPANY
LOS ANGELES, CALIFORNIA

Published by
HOLLOWAY HOUSE PUBLISHING COMPANY
8060 Melrose Avenue, Los Angeles, CA 90046

International Standard Book Number 0-87067-865-5
Printed in the United States of America

Cover photograph by Jeffrey
Cover design by Paul M. Papp

WHEN WE PRACTICE TO DECEIVE

Chapter 1

"Damn. Run us over next time," Barbara said aloud to the woman who crossed in front of them, forcing her and Monica to stop abruptly. "She didn't even turn around. People don't have any man.... Monica? Why are you standing back there with your mouth open?"

"That was my cousin," Monica said, watching the woman dash across the street.

"Who?"

"There," she said, pointing at the woman now on the other side of the street.

"Are you...?"

"DeeAnn! DeeAnn!" Monica suddenly called out.

Though only fleetingly, the woman had turned.

Monica saw clearly the startled look on her face. Immediately, the woman turned back into the street, stepping into the path of an oncoming gypsy cab which screeched to a stop just inches from her.

"DeeAnn!" Monica shouted, starting to step off the

curb herself but was pulled back by Barbara just as a car passed in front of her.

"Girl, you better watch it," Barbara said.

Running around the cab, the woman pulled open the rear door on the passenger side and threw herself inside. The cab pulled off.

"What, is she deaf?"

"Is a bat?" Monica asked, watching the woman in the cab shield her face with her hand.

"Then maybe this is one of those cases of mistaken identity," Barbara said, holding her shoulder bag closer to her side to keep it from dangling whenever someone passed too close to her. "I mean the woman that got into that cab was white."

"Look," Monica said, planting her left hand on her hip and looking up into Barbara's eyes. "I didn't make a mistake. I know I haven't seen DeeAnn in years, but I'd know her anywhere, even with blonde hair."

"Oh, it's like that. A little mixing of the bloods?"

"First cousins, honey," she said, looking in the direction the cab had gone.

"Not much family resemblance," Barbara said jokingly.

"How can you tell? She took off like a shot. Did you see her turn when I first called her?"

"Then if she saw you, why did she run?"

"Because we never got along and because she's funny acting that way. DeeAnn's behaving the same way she always did—like she don't want to be seen around family."

"Well from the glimpse I got of her, I can see where she might have an identity problem."

"It didn't have to be that way. My family is really kind

of close, and she grew up around us," Monica said, still looking down Court Street.

"So which parent is white?"

"Her mother. Her father is my mother's brother."

"Is she an only child?"

"No, she has a younger brother. Winston. Real good looking."

"Does she get along with him?"

"If getting along means acting like he doesn't exist, then yes. Actually, she treats Uncle Douglas and Winston like they were aliens from planet noir."

"Her own blood?" Barbara asked.

Monica turned away from the street and, looking at Barbara, nodded twice, her lips pursed.

"That's awful."

"Yes, it is. By now I would've thought that she would've gotten over her childhood confusion about her ethnicity."

Flipping her hand at Monica, Barbara said, "Problems grow up too. They get bigger and badder if they're not resolved."

"Yeah, well," Monica said, shaking her head slowly. "She's caused a lot of grief for her parents, and if she's still running, she must be causing a lot of grief for herself too."

"Only she knows," Barbara said, turning and looking at a girl walk past. "Will you look at that tight little skirt. Can it get any shorter?"

Monica looked but said nothing.

"I don't know how they come out of the house like that," Barbara said, looking again at Monica. "Are you okay? You look so sad."

Sighing softly and then sucking her teeth, she said,

"I'll be all right. I was just surprised to see DeeAnn. For an instant there, I forgot we didn't like each other and remembered only that we were kin. For some stupid reason I feel hurt."

"It's not stupid; you have feelings. Besides, I have plenty of relatives I don't like that I haven't seen in years who could still hurt my feelings. Oh look at you, all down in the dumps. Girl, you just won your first acquittal. Don't let your wannabe cousin spoil it for you," Barbara said, looking at her watch. "I have to get back to court. I'll call you later, okay?"

Checking her own watch, Monica said, "I have to get back too. Thanks for lunch."

"Welcome, pal," Barbara said before rushing off to the Supreme Court building where she worked as a court reporter.

For an idle minute, Monica stood in the midst of the everyday bustling lunch crowd massaging her well-satiated stomach. She had eaten more than her fill of lasagna. It was a good thing her healthy appetite didn't tell on her.

A strange sadness washed over her as she began making her way back to the office. Skillfully sidestepping around people in front of her walking too slowly or coming at her with blinders on, she realized that she should have expected that DeeAnn would run at the sight of her. They had never been friends. And judging by the way she took off, a nodding acquaintance was out of the question even now.

Slight flutterings in her stomach reminded her of how much DeeAnn could always get to her, just as she had when they were both eleven years old and fought over a degrading remark she made to Kevin. Up until that moment, though they had never voiced their dislike for each other. Looking back, what happened was inevitable.

It was a Saturday morning back in 1971 and the music of Soul Train was sounding throughout the family room in the basement. DeeAnn and Winston, who'd just turned six, stayed with them whenever Uncle Douglas and Aunt Wendy both had to work at the auto factory, which DeeAnn was never too pleased about; she always seemed to be sulking.

It was while they were watching Soul Train that Kevin said, "I'm gonna grow my afro bigger then anybody on Soul Train." Smart-mouth DeeAnn chimed in, "All that hair's gonna make you look even more like a wild jungle bunny."

The words and DeeAnn's smugness touched a raw nerve. Actually DeeAnn had been getting on her nerves big time since school started up again. She had whined and whined about not liking the school until Uncle Douglas gave in and transferred her to another school outside the neighborhood. But the real deal was that DeeAnn wanted to go to a predominantly white school because that's where she thought she belonged. She didn't have any friends in her old school, not because no one wanted to be her friend, but because she didn't want to be friends with anyone black. She was always off by herself. When the other kids realized that she didn't speak to DeeAnn, they started teasing her and calling her 'half-breed' or 'white girl.' Although she didn't join in, as far as she was concerned, DeeAnn brought it all on herself, acting stuck up and all.

That's why, when DeeAnn opened her mouth and called Kevin a wild jungle bunny, she saw red. Kevin was a year older and could defend himself, though she

11

doubted he would have done what she did. She sprang up off the floor and charged at DeeAnn like a mad rhino. The weight and force of her body slammed DeeAnn and her chair back hard onto the floor. She saw wide-eyed fear scream in DeeAnn's hazel eyes before she was knocked over in her chair. Their bodies entangled, they wrestled on the floor, pulling at hair, clothes, body parts.

Winston cried. Kevin rooted her on. She didn't know how long they had tussled before her mother snatched them apart. They were both punished—sent off to separate rooms to sit quietly; no television, no music. She didn't cry, but DeeAnn did. Which was surprising because she always seemed so unemotional.

DeeAnn's coldness toward Uncle Douglas, Winston, and the family in general bothered her. At family gatherings DeeAnn would change her seat if Uncle Douglas or Winston sat down next to her. If anyone in the family dared speak to her, she'd look down at the floor or up at the ceiling. How or why DeeAnn was allowed to get away with such rudeness was a mystery to her. As for herself, if she entered a room and didn't speak and adults were present, her mother would scold her. Whereas, no one said anything to DeeAnn.

Since the day of their big fight in the basement, they had not spoken. At family gatherings where they were both required to attend, they were quite adept at avoiding eye contact or getting too close to each other. The last time she saw DeeAnn was in Hudson's Department Store in downtown Detroit. She'd just returned home from graduating Howard University, and DeeAnn had graduated from the University of Michigan. She saw DeeAnn before DeeAnn saw her and stopped in front of her, blocking her way.

"Still perpetrating a fraud, Miss Dee?"

DeeAnn's face had flushed but she was cool; she never said a word. She never missed a step. Expressionless, DeeAnn had stepped around her and walked on, her head held high, her walk straight and determined.

Soon after, DeeAnn left Detroit and she hadn't thought much about her until she saw her just now. And as always, it was the fickleness of fate that played such a cruel game and had them both in the same city. That is, if DeeAnn was living in New York. Aunt Wendy and Uncle Douglas didn't seem to know for sure where DeeAnn called home.

"Congratulations, Monica."

"Thanks," she responded, stopping at Ellen's desk.

"How does it feel to be a winner?"

"Like I got all 'A's in my course work."

"'A' is for acquittal."

"Yes, but it's only as good as the last trial. The next trial is a new beginning. Speaking of which, did Rufus Washington's mother return my call?"

Chapter 2

"Carroll Street between Seventh and Eighth!" Nancy shouted from the back of the cab before she slammed the door closed. God, when she heard her old name called out, she almost dropped dead. No one in New York knew her as DeeAnn Taylor.

"What's wrong with you, lady? You trying to get yourself killed? 'Cause if'n you are, obliging you with my car ain't on my agenda today," the cab driver said, half turned in his seat, the fleshy wrinkles prominent on his weathered old black forehead.

"I'm late for an appointment," Nancy snapped, while looking furtively through the side window to see if Monica was coming after her.

Normally, she would never have gotten into a gypsy cab—after all, a criminal could be behind the wheel. The law didn't require gypsy cab drivers to have their pictures and license numbers facing the passengers, because it was illegal for them to be operating as a taxi service in the first place. Then, too, going home in the middle of the day on the spur of the moment wasn't normal either.

"Everybody's always in a hurry. I ain't picked up one fare today that wasn't in a hurry. I gotta get outta this always-in-a-hurry city. Everybody's living fast and dying young in New York. Kids no older then day-old bread selling drugs and killing like they hired by the mob. Kids shouldn't be born in New...."

"Can this be closed?" Nancy asked, referring to the badly scratched cloudy plexiglass divider atop the back of the front seat.

The driver glanced back at her. "It's broken."

"Then, if you don't mind, I'd rather ride in silence."

Through the rearview mirror, Nancy and the driver locked eyes for a brief second. If he was about to say anything else, he thought twice about it. Looking back at the road ahead, he sped down Court Street and made a right turn onto Tillery Street.

For a moment, Nancy's eyes stayed on the back of the driver's head. His wooly black hair was heavily sprinkled with gray that was more faded yellow than white. What's worse, to her it looked like mangy dog hair. Looking away and screwing up her face like she'd gotten a whiff of rotten fish, Nancy started to settle back, when she noticed the filthy gray vinyl she was sitting on. Just about anyone could've sat back here she guessed, hoping that none of the scum would rub off onto her tan linen suit. Balancing her pocketbook and briefcase on her lap, she continued to sit up straight by holding onto the door handle to maintain her balance. A cool breeze from the open front windows made her shiver and remember that, since it had turned out to be such a clear May day after the early morning showers, she had left her trench coat in the office when she went out for lunch.

In the office is where she ought to be, doing paperwork as she had planned, but she could not risk being seen by Monica returning to her office less than a block away.

Seeing Monica brought back all the horrors of who she really was. It had been easy to forget that somewhere inside her body there were genes, Douglas' bad genes, that held her black ancestry. Those genes were buried way down deep inside, because her mirror reflected only the white ancestry that made up her being—both physically and emotionally. For the past eight years, her mirror told her daily that she was Nancy Michaels, and as long as she stayed away from her family and anyone who had known her as a child, she would always be Nancy. To her co-workers in the DA's office, she was Nancy Michaels. To her few acquaintances and to Robert Willeton, she was Nancy Michaels.

If she could have changed who her father was as easily as she changed her name, she would have done it long ago. Then there would have been no need to tell herself that her real father was a white man. The fact that she had Douglas' full lips and high cheekbones disputed that belief, however. Fortunately for her, the current fad of silicone injections to give white girls fuller lips and fat implants in the cheeks to make them higher or fuller helped her to lose her self-consciousness about her face. But the truth was, even with her white skin, she looked more like Douglas than Wendy.

However, as long as she was never seen with Douglas, no one would ever guess that she was his daughter. She planned never to be seen with him again. Having to explain who he was when he picked her up after school once when she was in the third grade was humiliation enough. Both the white and black kids wanted to know who he was, and she was too ashamed to say that he was her father. It was easier to lie and say that he worked for her father. She refused to walk with him and ran off ahead, crying all the way home. Later that evening she heard Douglas tell Wendy, "I think DeeAnn's ashamed that I'm her father."

"You're imagining things," Wendy had responded.

"I don't think so," he said. "The child acted like I was a stranger."

"She might've been upset about something that happened in school."

"Then she should've been glad to see me."

"You know how kids are."

"What? Only a mother can comfort a child."

He never came for her again. Whether he physically came for her or not, she carried him with her everywhere; his black blood trickled through her veins. Throughout high school, she worried that the black girls might guess that she was part black. Staying clear of them had not been a hard decision to make. She was careful not to make any close white friends either, because she couldn't share her life. Yet there were times she wished that she had a best girlfriend to shop with, gossip with, or even talk about boys to. The reality was, what white boy or girl could she bring home anyway? She was not willing to find out how either would react to her parents.

There was no one to relate to. Everyone they knew was black, and there were no other interracial couples

17

or bi-racial children in their circle of existence. Wendy reminded her of an Oreo cookie—a white face surrounded by black people. She often wondered how Wendy lived without her people, her family, the friends she grew up with. How is it that she was able to give up everyone and everything to live among people who were so different from herself? That was not the life Nancy wanted to live; she wanted to live among people who looked like herself. She did not want to stand out; she wanted to blend in. No one had to know that she was tainted.

"Lady, if you don't mind, I have to make a living. I can't sit here with you all day daydreaming. Where do you want me to stop?" the driver asked, his irritation obvious.

"Oh. Sor.... Stop by that blue car. How much?"

"Eight dollars."

Scrounging around in her change purse and coming up with a five dollar bill, two singles and four quarters, Nancy reached through the opening in the plexiglass shield and said curtly, "Here." She dropped the wad of bills and coins onto the front seat before the driver had a chance to reach for it. Hoisting herself out of the back seat she stumbled when the heel of her shoe caught on the tattered carpet. Catching herself, she slammed the door shut.

"Bitch," the old man said before pulling out quickly from the curb.

Without giving the cab a backwards glance, Nancy ran up the brownstone stairs and let herself into the building. Once inside her second floor apartment, she went immediately to the phone and dialed her office.

"Jean? This is Nancy. I have a family emergency that's

keeping me longer than I expected. I won't be back in the office today."

"Should I check your calendar?"

"No. I have nothing pressing this afternoon. If anyone should ask for me, just tell them that I went over to the law library, okay?"

"Sure."

"Oh, and Jean, if someone name Monica…, never mind," she said. Monica wasn't going to call because she would be looking for DeeAnn Taylor, not blonde Nancy Michaels. "I'll see you tomorrow. Bye."

Placing the phone carefully back into its cradle, Nancy looked around her traditionally furnished peach and white living room. Some of the pieces were antiques she and Robert rescued from used furniture shops and flea markets. They had paid dearly to have these pieces refurbished. Absentmindedly stroking the top of the mahogany end table that felt as smooth and cool as satin, she was glad that cost had not been an issue.

This was the home she had made with Robert Willeton for the past three years. From the start, he had been told that her parents had both died in an automobile accident when she was five years old and that her spinster Aunt Amy had raised her in Lansing, Michigan, and had herself died of cancer in 1984. She had been careful to center her life in Michigan because forgetting places was too easy a thing to do. She convinced Robert that she was all alone in the world and he, as well as his Irish-American Connecticut family, had accepted her as such. Marriage was more than a likelihood and Monica's presence in New York could interfere with that.

Not staying in touch with Wendy had its disadvantages—Wendy would have told her that Monica was here and why. Finding out if Monica lived in New York—more specifically Brooklyn—was important but not important enough for her to take the chance on calling home and becoming involved with the family again.

Stepping in front of the tall windows that looked down onto the street, Nancy hugged her body as if she wanted to shield herself from a chill. The brownstones across the street stood dark against the clear spring sky. Many had been renovated by young professional couples whose careers demanded that they get nannies or *au pair* girls for their children. They traveled, they dined, they lived the dream that so many black people could not even imagine. But she could imagine it and would live it. Except, she would not have the children.

High-school biology had taught her well about recessive traits and their nasty habit of skipping a generation and popping up in the next. Getting pregnant at twenty-two had scared her to death, and though she had to go through five doctors before she found one who would agree to doing a tubal ligation on her, it was done when she was twenty-four. She was not willing to take the chance that some tan-complexioned or white-looking kid with sandy colored, frizzy hair would call her mommy.

She and Robert had discussed children at the start of their relationship—he wanted children. She told him that she did too, but she also told him that she had an IUD. Once they were married and were unsuccessful at having children, she would tell him that the IUD rendered her infertile. Robert was smart though; he might entertain the idea of in vitro fertilization, but she would argue against starting a baby in a petri dish and convince him that adoption was the best option. Whatever had to be done to keep her secret and Robert, she would do.

Chapter 3

Sitting on cold coarse stone, her behind aching for a pillow, did nothing to ease Monica's preoccupation with DeeAnn. Instead of staying in the office working until seven as she had planned, she chucked everything and was on the bus to Dayton's house by six. He wasn't due home until eight, but if she had gone home, only an earthquake could have forced her out again. Besides, if Mr. Hendricks was home, he would have let her in. But it wasn't until she was walking up Maple Street that she remembered that Thursday night was one of his lodge nights. Waiting would have to do, but it meant waiting with thoughts of DeeAnn.

It didn't seem to matter to anyone but Uncle Douglas that DeeAnn had distanced herself from the family. Aunt Wendy never said anything, but Uncle Douglas had a hard time masking his hurt. One of the few times he did discuss DeeAnn, he told her mother, Renee, that he felt like he'd never had a daughter. Though he teared when he said it, to him Winston was an only child. Renee said that Uncle Douglas, even as a child, was never one to upset the applecart. He always figured that problems would eventually work themselves out. But he must not have felt that way back in 1959 when he married Wendy O'Brian. Seems he more than upset the applecart; he turned it over. That alone was proof that he had an inner strength deeper and stronger than he let the world see. He had to be strong to survive the disapproval of both races.

Regardless of her own feelings on the subject of inter-racial marriages, Renee never spoke against her brother and his choice of a white woman for a wife. She always said that was his choice, but it would never be hers.

One afternoon when she was seventeen, she overheard Renee girl-talking with her best friend, Miss Maxine. Renee said, "…the only thing a white man could do for her was point her in the direction of a black man." Miss Maxine had then said, "Make sure he's tall, dark, and strapped." They cracked up laughing behind that. Forgetting that she could be heard out in the hallway, she had ha haed and tee-heed too loudly and got caught. She was slapped upside the head for listening to adult conversation. The next time she eavesdropped, she kept her mouth shut.

"Hi, babe, I wasn't expecting you 'til eight. You been waiting long?"

"Dayton. I didn't see you come up," Monica said, bending to scoop up her briefcase, which had slipped off her lap when she jumped to her feet.

"I parked right in front of you. Something bothering you about one of your cases?" he asked, taking his house keys from his front pants pocket as he came up the stairs.

Before unlocking the door, he bent down and kissed Monica on the lips.

"I'm not worried, but the Rufus Washington murder case starts Monday."

"Are you ready to defend?"

"Not really. Mr. Evans is still in South Carolina following up on a lead. What I need is a witness who can prove that, although Rufus did fight with the deceased that night, she was alive when he left the apartment."

Locking the door behind them, Dayton took off his trench coat and hung it on a coat hook in the hallway.

"Let me take your coat. How do you feel about this case?" he asked, hanging up Monica's coat and then leading the way up to his second-floor apartment. His father lived on the first floor alone since his second wife died a year ago.

"Let's just say, I believe Rufus. There have been no inconsistencies in his story and believe me, I've tried tripping him up several times. Sure, he's rough and he's street, but I don't think he killed Charlene Madison. He likes women. A man who likes women doesn't hit them or kill them."

"Says who?"

"Says me," Monica said, putting down her briefcase.

"Go ask that woman whose husband never hit her once in thirty years but tried to kill her over whether or not they should have a real tree for Christmas."

"Dayton, who knows what happened in those thirty years. Besides, thirty years don't say that he liked her."

"I wouldn't stay with someone I didn't like."

"Neither would I, but people do it every day. Still, I see Rufus as a man who'd walk before he'd let himself hit a woman. Plus, he speaks fondly of his mother and

23

Charlene, not like some clients who call the women in their lives bitches, broads, and whores."

"How old is he?"

"Twenty-three. He seems to be really concerned about how all of this is affecting his mother," Monica said in defense of her client, while lowering her tender behind down onto the hard, brown-twill sofa in the living room.

As many times as she'd been in Dayton's apartment, she was always struck by the bareness of the walls and the boxy pillowless sofa, which reminded her of a doctor's waiting room. Definitely needs a woman's touch in here. Neat enough but absolutely no color. Then again, that wasn't her problem. She wasn't about to get all involved in decorating and playing the "I could be the perfect wife" game. No one was going to accuse her of sending out "marry me please, I'm desperate" signals.

"Rufus should've thought about his mother before he got in trouble."

"You're assuming that he's guilty."

"If he's not, then he put himself in a situation where he's perceived to be guilty."

"Anyone can be in the wrong place at the wrong time, including you and me," she responded, glimpsing a sparkle in Dayton's eyes. He always seemed to get a kick out of debating her.

"I disagree. As a child I might've ended up where I wasn't supposed to be. But as a man, no way."

"You don't know that."

"Yes I do," he said, self-assuredly.

"Then you're very fortunate if you can tell fate not to step onto your path."

"I can. I control my destiny, not chance."

"You're not getting me into that debate. Don't even

24

try it," Monica said, squinting her eyes and pointing her finger threateningly at Dayton.

"Well, that's how I feel."

"Look, you have experience behind you. Rufus has a ways to go. It's no secret that he's uneducated and hangs with a rough crowd. I'm just saying that I don't feel uncomfortable around him. I have a good feeling about him."

"I understand some of the most notorious serial killers have been great charmers. I hope you have solid facts to back up your intuition," Dayton said, before going off into his den to put down his oversized brown briefcase and to take off his suit jacket.

Stunned, Monica glared through the doorway into the den, where she caught glimpses of Dayton moving about. Boldly folding her arms across her chest, she said, "I want it on record that I take exception to your supercilious remark and to your lack of confidence in my professionalism. I will not argue whether or not my defense is based on fact or intuition or both. I am a good attorney and I take exception to your doubting that fact."

Rushing back into the room, Dayton said quickly, "Time out. I didn't say you weren't a good attorney. And I'm not doubting your professionalism. I only meant that you shouldn't let your client's obvious charm cloud your perspective."

"Please, I do not…. Wait, let me put it this way. When you told me about a particular sixteen-year-old student who was deemed incorrigible and unteachable by every teacher in your school and, no matter how many teachers pressured you as principal to expel him, you hung tough and searched for a program that you felt would turn him around. When you found none, you started Kids

25

In Need Of Guidance, which you said could help kids who could not make it in regular classes, because they were not properly schooled by their parents or their previous teachers. You felt that it wasn't too late to step in and reeducate this boy from elementary to high school."

"Yes, but this kid was in school."

"So. He was a problem. Even your colleagues told you that you were wasting your time. But you told them you had a gut feeling this program could save that kid and so many others like him. You fought until the Board of Education supported you. You went on instinct, experience, and knowledge. Two years later, your program is a success. Your star pupil is the very one that everyone had given up on, and there's talk of integrating this program in other high schools in this city. It was what you felt for that boy that got you going in the first place. That boy could have just as easily been Rufus Washington," Monica concluded, sitting back and crossing her legs.

Though his thick mustache hid most of his upper lip, she could see clearly his roguish smile.

"You can wipe that smile off your face."

Stepping around the coffee table, he sat down next to her.

Monica looked away when he tried to look into her eyes.

Placing his left arm on the back of the sofa around her shoulders, Dayton moved his right hand slowly up and down her arm. "I love your lips when you're pouting."

She drew her lips in.

"I apologize, baby. You're right. I admit that intuition and knowledge can go hand-in-hand. Except the prob-

26

lem I find with this, hum…, let's say, this intuition business is that women claim exclusive rights."

Turning and looking at him, her face just inches from his, Monica asked, "You jealous?"

"No. A man doesn't need intuition, he operates on knowledge, skill, and wit," he said, exhaling once on the fingertips of his right hand and rubbing them on his chest as if to shine his nails.

"Sure, right. Tell me another."

Dayton chuckled.

"Look at it this way, Dayton. If you were accused of murder and you claimed justifiable homicide—self-defense, temporary insanity or even plain old not guilty—would you not want the attorney on your case to believe in you and defend you to the utmost of his or her ability?"

"Without question."

"Then how can you question my belief in my client?"

"I'm not. I'm just saying that everyone isn't innocent."

"No, but if you're the one who is, you would want your attorney to believe in you and knock down all the roadblocks."

"Okay, okay. You win," Dayton said, putting up his hands in surrender. "I stand corrected. So if it's not this case, what had you so preoccupied when I came up?"

"I don't wanna talk about that right now," she said, letting her head roll back onto his arm.

Looking down into Monica's eyes and again rubbing her arm, Dayton slid out the tip of his tongue and briefly touched the left edge of his mustache.

Monica stared at his mouth even after his tongue disappeared. When she looked up into his eyes, her body warmed.

Lowering his lips to hers, he kissed her gently before easing his tongue inside her. She tasted him. She moaned.

"Baby, I know how you feel," Dayton said, pulling away. "If we get started, it's all over."

"Oh, you're mean."

"Am I?" Dayton teased, kissing her again, and again pulling away. "Let's not get too comfortable. I promised to take you out to dinner, plus I have a lot of paperwork to do this evening."

"You're right. Tonight, work first," Monica said, sitting up straight. "I could pass on dinner; I had a big lunch. Besides, I'd rather celebrate Saturday night."

"Sounds good to me," Dayton agreed, pushing himself off the low sofa and straightening up to his full six foot two inches.

"What about your dinner?"

"No problem. I can finish off the baked chicken I made yesterday," he said over his shoulder before leaving the room.

"Oh, before I forget. When I clear Rufus, will you help him get into an accredited GED program?" she asked loud enough for him to hear her two rooms away in the kitchen.

"Sure. Only if you tell me what's on your mind when I come back in there."

Chapter 4

Pacing from the stove to the kitchen door, wringing her hands and peeking down the hall towards the bedroom, Nancy listened for sounds of Robert moving about. Having been out of the bathroom fifteen minutes, he called her once to ask if she wanted to meet him at the health club after work. If time permitted, he worked out three to four days a week at the fitness center a few blocks away. He was steadfast in his belief that a toned, taut body and the right clothes were a man's best advertisement for health and success. Upon turning thirty-five this past March, Robert escalated his workout routine. He lifted weights, did aerobics, and jogged four days a week. He could've given Hollywood's best hunks a run for their money on his worst day. He was tall, he was handsome, he was hers.

Basically, Nancy was lazy about working out. She kept up with her aerobics and stretching to please Robert. She had a good body, more hips and butt than she would've asked for, but everything was tight and in proportion. Robert had no problems smiling when she walked around the house naked; he got an erection every time. Sex with him was satisfying, though she ached to tell him to touch her clitoris more—that's what made her toes curl. Last night they had not made love because she had pretended to be swamped with office work. Her eyes were on the pages of a law book, but her mind was on Monica. Luckily for her, Robert was just as involved with his work. She had waited until he was asleep before she went to bed, but she didn't sleep through the night.

A dream she had frequently dreamed before she left home awakened her. In the dream she was always lying in darkness, an invisible, unbearable weight paralyzing her legs, while she gasped for breath. She sensed that she was in a vacuum—no air, no light; but there was constantly an indistinguishable sound around her. Staying in bed as long as she could, she finally got up at five. She had sat in the bathtub, shriveling up like an old lady, until six-thirty, the time she usually got up. She could not keep avoiding Robert; not much got past him.

"Robbie, do you want orange juice while the coffee's brewing?" she asked from the doorway of the bedroom.

"No thanks. I'll wait for the coffee," he answered from inside the large walk-in closet they shared. "I'll be out in a minute. I can't find my blue and red Italian silk tie; it's not on the tie rack. Have you seen it?"

"Look behind the door. I hung another rack there two days ago to accommodate your strays. I can't imagine how you found anything the way all those ties were all bunched up and entangled."

Barely audible behind the closed door, Robert called out, "Thanks, Nance. I was meaning to get another rack."

Walking softly across the room, Nancy sat at the foot of the neatly made up double bed. Robert was good about making the bed if he was the last one up. In fact, he was as much of a neatnik as she was, except when it came to his ties and socks. It was like a free-for-all in his sock drawer. He didn't like them tied together or turned inside each other like a ball. He liked them folded together and placed neatly in the drawer, but by the time he rummaged through them, none were left with their matches. Maybe that's the way he expressed his sloppy side. Every other aspect of his life was strictly organized, categorized, planned. He left nothing to chance; she liked that about him and pretty much existed the same way.

They met on a Sunday afternoon in early July in the Brooklyn Botanic Gardens. They were both standing on the deck in the Japanese garden looking out onto the pond. Robert remarked to her about the idyllic scene around them and they started talking. They spent the rest of the afternoon strolling through the gardens. It was perfect. At first she was afraid that Robert might sense that she was mixed-race and run for the hills in disgust. He didn't.

Six and a half months later, they found an apartment together in Park Slope where they were both already living. She loved him. He could give her the life she wanted. No other man fulfilled her as Robert did. The two others she'd allowed herself to get involved with had been weak, unambitious, and average. Nancy wanted a man with a future; she would not settle for just anyone, and Robert was not just anyone. He had vision: in two years, he planned on being a partner at Rose, Mendelshon and White. He wanted a colonial style house in New Bedford, Connecticut, and a summer home in Menemsha on Martha's Vineyard. She intended to be his wife when he realized his dreams.

Robert came out of the closet wearing one of his Giorgio Armani suits, which meant that he was meeting with an important client or one of the law partners. He loved his job and the future it promised. He never understood why she opted for criminal law and the DA's office, even after she had explained that the mix of female corporate attorneys and the old boy network were like oil and water. What Nancy hadn't said was that her life was hard enough keeping her parentage a secret; she could not risk that the corporate big boys would look into her background. She had wanted to be a lawyer since she was fifteen and intoxicated by reruns of Perry Mason. Her plan was to work in the DA's office for five years, then seek a partnership in private practice catering, hopefully, to white people with money. They, too, needed criminal lawyers.

"Tell me, what's keeping a lifelong member of the Rip van Winkle fan club awake? When I closed my eyes around midnight you were deep in the books, and you were up before the sun this morning."

"I just wasn't sleepy last night, that's all," she said as nonchalantly as possible, crossing her legs to still the shaking that always came when she was nervous. She prayed that her voice would not give away the panic she felt.

"That's a rarity, you not sleepy," he said, looking at her reflection in the dresser mirror while expertly tying his tie. "What were you working on?"

"Just research."

"Hmmmm. Oh yes, and before I forget, Ellen and

Peter have invited us to join them at the Provence in Soho next Friday evening for dinner. I told them, tentatively, we're available. All right with you?"

"Fine. What's the occasion?"

"Nothing special. You know Ellen can't cook, so they're probably reciprocating for that dinner you cooked last month. They're paying."

"I'm looking forward to it," she lied. Socializing was an effort for her, but for Robert, as always, she would wear a nice dress and a nice smile. Robert and Peter would talk stocks, bonds, and trading all evening, while Ellen would ask too many personal questions. As much as she could, she would steer their conversations toward clothes, decorating, jewelry.

"I'll be back," he said, going back into the bathroom.

As for cooking, she certainly didn't learn at home. While in law school, to keep herself from starving and spending all of her money in restaurants, she took two cooking courses and invested in a few good cook books. If she had to say so herself, she was a darn good cook— French and Italian cuisine her better efforts. When time permitted, she served up a delicious seven-course meal for Robert. He was worth the time and effort.

However, telling Robert the truth about her family was something she could never do. Their life together was well-rooted in the white world. Neither one of them knew any blacks personally and she never socialized with anyone from her job. Other than a cursory mention about the blacks they saw on television news programs, there was rarely an occasion they had to discuss black people. Even then, if there was a threat of a prolonged discussion about black people, she'd quickly change the subject or, at times, initiate sex. Robert fell for it every time. There was no need to talk about black people or white people for that matter; after all, they were white and didn't have to spend time discussing who they were.

As an ADA, she prosecuted her share of the black criminals that paraded through the courts each day. Each and every one of them reinforced the shame she felt about having black blood in her veins. It was a personal pleasure to win a case, not so much for her career as it was to put as many blacks behind bars and off the streets as possible.

Although Robert never expressed any overt dislike for black people, she knew that she could never tell him that she was black. He would hate her for deceiving him and all would be lost. A queasiness gripped her stomach.

"You don't look too good. What's wrong?" Robert asked, stepping back into the room.

Nancy got up quickly and went to the doorway. "Thinking about the work I have to do this morning. I was up early because I have to help Margolis set up the new arraignment schedule for night court. I want to get to work no later than eight fifteen, if that's all right with you," she said, immediately regretting the sarcasm.

Arching his eyebrows, Robert turned to face her. "Hey. Don't bite my head off."

"I'm sorry."

"Something happening at work? You seemed a bit distracted last night and this morning; I don't know."

Mindful of speaking softly, she said, "I don't think I was distracted at all. And even if I was, I'm supposed to be a moody Capricorn remember, which means that I'm entitled once in a blue moon."

The moment the words were out of her mouth, she wished she hadn't said them. The words didn't sound right even to her own ears. Seeing the hurt in Robert's beautiful blue eyes made her feel worse. This was part of her fear: losing control.

"I'm sorry. I'm a little under the weather. I'll get your coffee," she said, dashing out of the room.

In the kitchen, placing both her hands on her hips, Nancy closed her eyes and let her head drop dejectedly to her chest. She had to get a grip on her emotions and her nerves. There was no way that Monica could come into her life and wreak havoc; she could do just as much damage herself out of fear, if she didn't stop worrying and being afraid.

Coming up behind her, Robert embraced her and held her close.

"I'm sorry Robbie. I don't know what came over me."

"When's your period due?"

"What?" she asked, pulling free of his embrace.

"I just asked. You know you get a little testy around that time."

"Forget it. I have to get to work."

"So do I. By the way, I might have to work late. I'll probably eat out."

"But Robert, earlier you asked me to meet you at the fitness center after work."

"My mistake. I forgot about a meeting scheduled for six. No telling how long it'll last."

"That's the third time this week. For the past five months, you've had to work late."

"And I've explained that negotiations on the Alcoa/Warner merger are complex and time-consuming. It'll be a while yet before all the wrinkles are ironed out."

"Fine," she said, leaving Robert in the kitchen,

annoyed that he was spending an excessive amount of time on the job and that, like most men, he blamed female emotions on the ever-convenient period. If only it was simply her period that was bothering her, she thought, while gathering up her briefcase and pocketbook from the living room sofa.

On her way out of the apartment, stopping once to look at herself in the hall mirror, Nancy checked her skin for blemishes and any sign of a tan. Summer was a month away, yet the sun was already hot. It was a mystery to her that white people wanted to turn brown.

The end of their getaway weekend had come all too soon, though the sensual sweetness lingered. The long uninterrupted hours of lovemaking on Martha's Vineyard had calmed the dread that had consumed her all day Friday. Loving thoughts of Robert and his concern that she was overworked and needed a change of scenery brought a smile to Nancy's face as she sat at her desk absentmindedly flipping through the pages of one of the files in front of her. Maybe it was all a fluke that Monica happened to be at that particular street corner at that particular time. The law of probability was against their paths crossing again, especially since she never intended to go back home. All that worry had been for nothing.

"How you doing there, Nancy?"

"Oh, hi, John."

"How was your weekend?"

Something was up. John was flashing that false "I'm going to make you do something you don't want to do" smile. As her immediate supervisor, John Margolis never made small talk. He was a stickler for office rules and regulations and every case had to be argued by the book.

Behind his back everyone called him the "Margolian Dictator." John wanted something from her now, and he was going to get it. No ifs, ands, or buts.

"My weekend was great. Robert and I went up to Martha's Vineyard. It's really beautiful this…."

"Look, I know you're working on the Cummings case, but I'm gonna have to put you on the Rufus Washington murder trial, which begins today. Irv Weinstein's case in Supreme Court had some unexpected testimony that opened a Pandora's box. It looks like it's gonna run a few weeks more. Here's the file; you have ten minutes to go over it. You're due in criminal court in Jury Six in fifteen minutes before Judge DeLeone."

Her first impulse was to say hell no, but her better sense kicked in. This was no time to be on the Margolian Dictator's black list. She tried instead to reason.

"I can't just step in in the middle of the case. Irv never discussed Rufus Washington with me; I wouldn't know where to begin. Is the case winnable? What's my approach?"

By the impatient expression on his face, she knew that John wasn't buying her malarkey. She hated taking over someone else's case.

"The trial starts today, which is not the middle of the case according to my estimation. Judge DeLeone is not willing to delay another two weeks. And as for you not knowing anything about this case, you are an attorney well versed in criminal law, are you not? It'll take you no time to familiarize yourself with the particulars. Irv says that this is an open-and-shut case. Washington was the last one seen with the decedent that night and he can be placed in the apartment building around the time of death. Guilty written all over this case."

"I just meant that I'm not prepared to go before the court," she said, lowering her voice.

"Let's see," he said, leafing through the thick folder. "All pretrial motions and orders have been completed and filed by both sides; all subpoenas have been issued; evidence of proof and other investigative findings and witnesses duly compiled; the jury has been selected and seated; and defense attorney has rejected offers of a plea bargain. What else is there for you to do but appear?"

"Hummm, I...."

"Appear before Judge DeLeone and request a forty-eight-hour continuance so that you might acquaint yourself with your witnesses and evidence. Under the circumstances, I am sure Judge DeLeone will be amenable to such a delay; it has already been discussed. If you need to consult with me, you know where I am. Miss Michaels?"

"Yes?"

"You've already wasted five minutes."

Dropping the file on her desk, Margolis, without so much as a good-bye or good luck, strutted off. Probably off to make someone else's life miserable, Nancy thought.

"Don't look so put out; he was really kinda nice to you and you know it," Ross Whitney said from across the room.

"Imagine if he was angry with me," she said, smiling faintly.

Ross was the only other person in the office she shared with three other ADAs. They both knew that it was a waste of time to discuss what had just happened; they had no say in case selections. Throwing up her hands as if to say, "what can you do," she hurriedly shoved the file folder into her briefcase; retrieved her pocketbook from the desk drawer; and before bounding out of the office, plucked her trench coat off the coat rack near the door. The forecast had called for rain this afternoon.

Chapter 5

They'd been waiting just five minutes for the ADA to appear, yet by the general fidgetiness and mumbling throughout the courtroom, the wait seemed a lot longer and was made worst by the high humidity in the room. Apparently it was too early in the season to turn on the air conditioner.

Trying to use the ADA's tardiness to review her opening argument, Monica was distracted by a nervous Rufus Washington, who was sitting next to her to her left, steadily tapping on the table with one of her ballpoint pens. He was staring straight ahead at the judge's bench. Little wonder what was on his mind. Rufus was a good-looking young man, and he was dressed neatly in a cheap charcoal gray suit, white cotton shirt, and a solid navy blue tie—probably the most conservatively dressed he'd been in his life.

Rufus' mother, seated behind them in the first row, was quietly reciting the 27th Psalm. Mrs. Washington—

"Mrs." although she had never been married—appeared older than her forty-two years—perhaps used up by life or the lack of a life. She was born to the welfare system herself and raised her children on welfare. Like their mother, not one of her three girls or Rufus made it through high school—each of the girls had babies and their own welfare budgets.

Before his arrest, Rufus had worked as an apprentice of sorts for a small neighborhood general contractor, Mr. Whitney, who came forward as a character witness. Charlene had wanted Rufus to get his high-school diploma and, since he liked plumbing and carpentry, had been looking into trade schools that specialized in those areas. "Why would I kill Charlene?" he had asked, "She was the first girlfriend I ever had that thought I could be somebody."

Rufus was angry about her death and was adamant about testifying. He wanted to tell the judge and jury that, although he and Charlene had argued that night in September after leaving the house party, he did not kill her. He loved her.

It was what happened at the party that caused them to argue in the first place. He had noticed one too many times, that Charlene and a dude named Flash had danced one too many dances and that Charlene didn't seem to mind Flash holding her more than a little too close. During one dance, he caught Flash kissing Charlene on the neck. Rufus had snatched Flash—taller though not as burly as himself—off of Charlene and had punched him in the face. "The man wus disrespectin me," Rufus explained. The ensuing fight had been brutal; furniture was toppled and broken; the party was "turned out." Rufus admits that he wanted to kill Flash but never

Charlene. What he didn't know at the time, however, was that Flash was known to carry a gun. Fortunately, everyone had been body-searched at the door for weapons. Rufus denied owning a gun himself.

After arriving at Charlene's apartment six blocks away and finding that her mother and younger sister were still out, they continued to argue. Charlene had declared that nothing had happened, that the dances were no big deal, but Rufus wasn't convinced. He thought she liked Flash feeling her up. Regardless, Rufus swore that he never hit her and that he definitely never put his hands around her neck.

The coroner put the time of death between twelve thirty and one thirty A.M. Sunday morning, September 24, 1989. Rufus said that it was around one o'clock in the morning when Charlene kicked him out of the apartment. He remembers slamming the door when he left, sending an earsplitting bang ricocheting throughout the three-story brownstone.

From the floor above, Brendalynn Lenox had shouted, "Cut out that goddamn noise down there! It's one o'clock in the damn morning! I'll call the cops on your black asses y'all keep it up!"

By the time she was slamming her own door, Rufus was out of the building. He was sure that he heard the click of the lock behind him before he stepped away from the door, but Miss Lenox, in her deposition, stated that she never saw or heard Charlene after Rufus slammed the door.

Rufus maintained that he was home, in bed, two blocks away by one fifteen. His mother confirmed his alibi. Charlene's younger sister, Kisha, upon returning home with her mother at five thirty A.M., discovered her

42

body curled up on the floor of the closet they shared.

Rufus naively believed testifying under oath that he was innocent would immediately exonerate him. Monica let him have his dream; she didn't want to disillusion him. Her job was to give him the best possible legal defense at her disposal. However, insufficient evidence and reasonable doubt would be the determining factors in deciding the verdict. Which was why Mr. Evans was still in Charleston looking for Delroy "Flash" Brown. It was his mother who finally told Mr. Evans that Flash had left unexpectedly for South Carolina to visit family—a visit long overdue by nine years. His hasty departure was suspicious even to his own mother. Flash was the killer as far as Rufus was concerned, yet there was no evidence to back up his allegation. If they were going to find anything, it had better be soon.

Monica gently placed her left hand over Rufus' right hand to still the tapping. The waiting was taxing her too, and she hoped that Judge DeLeone, waiting in his chambers, was just as peeved as she was. More than likely he was. Judges had no problem having attorneys wait for them but would gladly show who the boss is if they were kept waiting. Still, it was rare for an ADA up against a Legal Aid attorney to raise the ire of a judge. That would be a real switch, as it was common knowledge that most judges were generally impatient with legal aid attorneys, for no reason other than that they were Legal Aid attorneys it seemed.

She was never sure if it was the caliber of attorneys the judges perceived that they were, working non-profit and all, or the caliber of the clients they represented that the judges did not like. Of course, there were the few seasoned mavericks who stood out, winning acquittal after acquittal, commanding respect from the judges. However, on the whole, Legal Aid attorneys were spoken to by most judges like they were high-school graduates instead of law-school graduates. It was subtle—the jury and the courtroom observers might not see it, but *they* did.

The young black court officer who had been standing at rest outside the judge's chambers suddenly turned and opened the door, sticking his head inside.

Just as suddenly, a woman swept down the aisle, sat down at the prosecutor's table, threw open her brief case, and after pulling out a thick file folder, wiggled out of her coat and laid it across the back of the chair next to her.

Monica's mouth fell open.

It was DeeAnn.

The hair was indeed blonde and the face was more mature, more woman than girl, but it was DeeAnn. The blonde hair really did the trick; no one would ever guess that she was anything but what she appeared to be.

Leaning sideways towards her, Monica whispered, "DeeAnn. Are you the ADA?"

Nancy's heart skipped a beat. Her breathing stopped. Her back stiffened. She could not bring herself to lift her eyes from the open file folder in front of her to look in the direction of the voice that called her. This couldn't be happening. She had never wanted to see her family again, especially Monica.

"DeeAnn."

Pulling her eyes away from the folder, Nancy slowly turned her head and looked into Monica's questioning eyes. Her heart pounded loudly in her chest. It *would* be the one person who had challenged her choices as a child who would appear in her life when everything was as she wanted it. Undoubtedly, Monica would challenge her choices now also. Her hands began to shake.

Startled by the panic leaping from DeeAnn's eyes, Monica stared at her. In all her life, she had never seen a person's complexion pallor instantly. DeeAnn looked as if she was about to faint.

"Are you all right?" she asked, getting up out of her chair to go over to her.

Nancy's eyes never left Monica's face. Her mind seemed to slow down. *She keeps calling me DeeAnn. That's not my name. Dear God, she's coming over here. She's going to tell everyone that I'm her cousin—that I'm black.* Beginning to hyperventilate, Nancy heard herself say, "I have to get out of here!"

A sudden weakness in her knees and trembling legs made getting to her feet awkward. Gripping the edge of the table, she tried to steady herself.

"My God, DeeAnn! What…?"

"All rise. This court is now in session. The Honorable Dominic P. DeLeone presiding. Docket number 41135/89. The People of the State of New York versus Rufus V. Washington."

Stepping backwards to her chair, Monica watched as DeeAnn appeared to waver, obviously holding onto the table for support.

Rushing from his chambers, Judge DeLeone sprinted up the few steps to his massive oak bench and plopped down in his oversized leather chair.

"Seat the jury, Mr. Whitman," Judge DeLeone ordered the court officer, who opened the door on the opposite side of the bench and paraded in the twelve jurors.

"Be seated!" the court officer announced, once the jurors were seated.

There was a hauntingly blank look on DeeAnn's face as she sank slowly back into her seat, still holding onto the table. Monica couldn't believe that seeing her had disturbed DeeAnn so severely.

"Miss Michaels, let us not have another incidence of tardiness during the course of this trial," Judge DeLeone admonished. Then to the court stenographer he said, "Nancy Michaels for the People."

Monica did a double take. "Who?"

Judge DeLeone's bushy salt-and-pepper eyebrows knitted tightly together when he leveled his piercing stare on Monica.

Placing her hand on her stomach, Nancy tried to halt the threat of the queasiness that was rising inside her.

"Miss Hall, do you have a question to put before this Court? The trial has not yet begun; are we overly anxious?"

"Oh, no sir, your honor. I beg your pardon," Monica responded quickly, glancing over at DeeAnn. No wonder she couldn't find a telephone number; the girl had changed her name.

Looking again at the ADA, Judge DeLeone asked, "Miss Michaels, do you and I understand each other?"

Nancy said nothing.

"Miss Michaels, if you'll tell us where you are, we'll all gladly join you," Judge DeLeone quipped.

Nancy belched and a sour liquid rose to her throat. Clamping her hands over her mouth, she jumped to her feet.

Monica was up out of her chair instantly.

Rumblings from confused spectators filled the courtroom.

Immediately standing also, Judge DeLeone banged his

gavel several times. "What in the world is going on here? Miss Michaels, are you sick? Are you about to throw up in my court?"

Nancy bobbed her head frantically. She didn't dare remove her hands.

"Mr. Whitman, show Miss Michaels into my chambers! Quickly!"

The court officer rushed immediately to Nancy's side; and with one hand on her left elbow, the other around her waist, he escorted her out of the room.

Monica started behind them.

"Miss Hall, where are you going?"

"Your honor, I thought perhaps I could assist…."

"No ma'am! Return to your seat! I don't know what's going on here, but you seem to be somewhat preoccupied yourself. I'm adjourning until nine o'clock Wednesday morning. Be ready to open without delay or incident. This court's adjourned," Judge DeLeone stated, banging his gavel twice and rushing from the courtroom, the jurors departing right on his heels.

An officer came over and handcuffed Rufus.

"Miss Hall, whut's up?" Rufus asked. "We can't start today?"

"Ummm, no. I'm sorry. We'll start in a few days. Don't worry; it's all right," Monica assured him as he was led from the room. He looked back at her a few times, but Monica was seated again and was quickly gathering up her papers. Her mind was on DeeAnn, who was probably in the judge's bathroom throwing up her breakfast.

She should barf up her heart while she was at it. What a bitch. She changed her name, is passing, and she got the nerve to be working in the DA's office. What a fraud.

It would devastate Uncle Douglas if he knew that DeeAnn had changed her name, and not through marriage.

The same feeling of rage that had consumed Monica when she was eleven years old held her captive again. But this time, she didn't want to beat DeeAnn up, she wanted to scream at her, "We come from a people that were the first on this earth! A people that built the pyramids; were favorites of God Almighty; and had the likes of Solomon, Moses and David to share our dark skin. So what that your skin is white! How dare you be ashamed of your father!" What in the world could have happened to make her turn her back on her blackness so early and bound her so completely?

Chapter 6

In the judge's private bathroom, down on her knees, her face inches above the pee-splashed porcelain, Nancy held her blouse close to her chest with her left hand while her right hand, pressed against the wall, kept her from falling face first into the toilet. She retched violently. There was nothing left in her stomach to bring up, it was the smell of stale pee that sickened her now. "Men are disgusting," she thought to herself. "The least they could do is wipe up after themselves." The knowledge that a successful white jurist could be ill-mannered enough to leave pee on the toilet, just as her black father had done back home in Michigan, was disconcerting. This was, apparently, one of those disgusting shared male frailties that knew nothing of skin color, she concluded, although Robert had never left evidence behind for her to discover.

As she attempted to get to her feet, another wave of nausea hit her. Her throat burned, her tongue tasted sour.

Finally letting go of the sink, Nancy flushed the toilet for the third time and, using the wall and sink for support, pulled her weakened body up off the floor. Tears flowed at the realization that Monica was responsible for reducing her to this level of degradation—on her knees, her face in a judge's toilet.

"Goddammit to hell! I despise you, you black bitch," she hissed.

Of all the courtrooms in this city, in this country, how could she and Monica have ended up within the same four walls? Her chest tightening from the rage welling up inside of her, Nancy came down hard on the sink with her fist, regretting it when pain shot through her right hand from the assault. Grimacing and holding her throbbing hand to her breast, Nancy caught sight of her tear-stained, flushed face in the mirror over the sink. Her eyes were red and swollen; she looked nothing like the woman she faced in her mirror this morning. That woman had still been glowing from a weekend of love and visions of a secure future. This woman into whose eyes she looked now was afraid of what the future might hold if Monica exposed her deception. Robert would surely find out.

She would have to get rid of Monica or relocate and give up her life in New York. But starting over elsewhere was not an option. Her life was here with Robert. The solution to this nightmare was to keep Monica quiet, but how could she do that? Money? Not a viable solution. Paying Monica to keep quiet was out of the question. She probably wouldn't take money because she would get a bigger thrill from seeing Nancy exposed and destroyed. Anyway, seventeen thousand dollars in savings and stocks might not be enough to buy Monica's silence, even if she could be bought. If she was anything like she was as a child, she couldn't be bought.

Even as a child, Monica had been haughtily self-assured. She never seemed to falter, no matter what it was she was doing or saying. She was like a little woman. Before they had stopped playing together, no matter what the game, Monica had to be the leader, the mommy, the teacher, in other words the grown-up. No one ever said she couldn't be. She always seemed to know who she was and what her reasons for being were, and she must have believed that one of those reasons was to drill into her her ethnic makeup. Monica never wasted an opportunity to tell Nancy that she was black. Monica, the woman, would undoubtedly be just as determined to force her opinions on her again. She was not going to go away like a puff of smoke. And being the tenacious bitch that she was, she was probably waiting out in the courtroom for her to return.

The bitter taste of Nancy's tongue reawakened her nausea. Using her left hand to pull a paper cup from the wall dispenser above the sink, Nancy filled it with cold water from the tap. Taking big gulps, she vigorously rinsed her mouth twice. Still, her mouth tasted pretty foul, her tongue felt thick and rough. Opening the judge's medicine cabinet she spotted a bottle of green mouthwash. Using the same cup, she took just enough to rinse and gargle the vomit taste from her mouth. The minty flavor refreshed her.

What could she say to Judge DeLeone? What in the world was she going to say if John Margolis found out? There was nothing in her legal training on how to handle this situation—throwing up in a judge's chambers. Maybe she could tell them both that she might be pregnant. God forbid. Forget that; it didn't pay to jinx herself. Tubal ligations were supposed to be the ultimate contraceptive, but one never knew for sure. Men who had vasectomies had been known to father children. She would have to say that it was probably something she ate, although she hadn't eaten a morsel all day. Or she could say that she had some bad milk with her coffee earlier.

Already her life was out of kilter. Changing her identity and beginning her life anew in New York City had been a simple matter compared to the stress she was now feeling and the lies she would have to tell if Monica blabbed. It had never entered her mind that Monica would make New York City her home too.

"I'm so stupid. This is no coincidence. Monica knew all along that I was in New York. Wendy had to have told her. I slipped and told her myself with my own big mouth. How could I be so stupid? The bitch came here to destroy me, and she was probably planning to do it right in front of Judge DeLeone. She could get me disbarred. Oh Lord, what am I going to do? Please God, make her disappear, vanish into thin air. Better still, let me wake up from this nightmare," she prayed, looking up to the ceiling.

"Tap…tap…tap."

The sudden knock at the door gave Nancy a start.

"Miss Michaels, are you all right in there? Do I need to summon a paramedic?" came Judge DeLeone's solicitous voice from the other side of the door.

"Ummmm, no sir," Nancy said, quickly combing through her hair with her fingers. "I'm fine now. I believe the milk I drank this morning didn't quite agree with my stomach."

52

"Are you sure? You didn't look too well."

Remembering her yoga, and using the cleansing breath technique, Nancy inhaled deeply and slowly exhaled before opening the door and facing Judge DeLeone. He did not look the stern jurist of his reputation.

"Thank you for your concern, sir. I beg your pardon and forgiveness for disrupting your courtroom."

"Things happen. However, this is the first time I've ever made a prosecutor sick to the stomach," Judge DeLeone teased.

Forcing a smile, Nancy responded, "You could never make anyone sick, sir. You're one of the finest jurists sitting in criminal court. Your reputation is that of fairness and a superior knowledge of the law."

"I guess that's why you prosecutors moan when a case is assigned to my court," he said with a little laugh.

Nancy felt her face flush.

"Don't look so serious. I'm not one to worry about what others think of me. What I hear about myself around here is quite laughable; what transpires in my courtroom is not. I've dismissed the court; you have a continuance until Wednesday morning. That should be enough time for you to get yourself and this case in shape."

"Thank you, your honor."

"The defense attorney was concerned for you; she's waiting in the courtroom."

"Your honor, if I might impose upon you once more?"

"Yes?"

"May I use the alternate exit from your chambers? I'm a little embarrassed; I really don't wish to see anyone."

"Of course you may, but didn't you leave your files

and personal belongings in the courtroom? I believe only Miss Hall is left out there; there's no need to be embarrassed." Taking Nancy's elbow, Judge DeLeone ushered her to the door that led to the courtroom and opened it. "I'll see you Wednesday morning at nine o'clock sharp."

"Yes sir, and thank you again, your honor," Nancy said meekly, feeling light-headed. This must be what it was like to be ushered into the gas chamber.

The door closed behind her.

Monica was waiting. Standing up as Nancy entered the courtroom, she asked, "Are you all right?"

Ignoring the question and Monica's presence, Nancy rushed over to the prosecutor's table. Snatching up the bulky case file, she stuffed it inside her briefcase.

"I know you may not want to talk to me, but we should talk," Monica said, taking a few steps towards Nancy, closing the small space between them.

Uncomfortable with Monica's nearness, Nancy yanked her coat off the back of the chair and started for the door.

Reacting quickly, Monica took off behind her and, grabbing her arm, pulled Nancy around to face her.

"Hey! Wait a minute. I'm talking to you."

"Get your black hands off me!" Nancy hissed, yanking herself free of Monica's grasp.

Throwing her hands up to show that she was no threat, Monica asked calmly, "The question of blackness is the problem you're having, isn't it? Am I to believe that you're pretending to not know me? Better yet, are you pretending to be someone else? Nancy Michaels?"

Glaring at Monica, Nancy spat, "I don't answer to you or anyone else on this earth!"

"No, I guess you don't. But tell me, is Nancy Michaels on your birth certificate?"

"Not that it's any of your damn business, my name is legally Nancy Michaels."

"Oh? Presto chango, huh?"

"Go to hell."

"No thanks, but you have my blessing."

Turning away sharply, Nancy started again for the door.

"We're not finished," Monica said, grabbing hold of Nancy's arm again and pulling her completely around, standing between her and the door. With her arms outstretched, she jumped to whatever side Nancy moved to prevent her from going around her.

"I feel like I'm a goddamn goalie for the New York Rangers. Will you please stand still for a minute? I only want to talk to you."

"Get the hell outta my way!"

"Wow. We are hostile, aren't we?"

"Get out of my way!"

"No lady, you don't walk away that easily. Okay, we'll play it your way. But tell me first, what's the name of the game you're playing? I'd like to know the rules. You're white, I'm black. You don't talk to black folks, relation or not."

"I'm warning you, get out of my way."

Monica didn't flinch. After all, a threat from DeeAnn never meant much. For a second they faced each other, both breathing deeply, their eyes locked.

Nancy was incensed. She hated Monica more than she thought possible. Monica's actions so enraged and frustrated her that, if she could've gotten away with it, she would've crushed Monica's skull with the rigid edge of her briefcase. Instead, she summoned all of her strength and, using her body, pushed Monica aside against the hard wooden bench.

Landing hard on her right hip, Monica rebounded quickly and grabbed the tail of Nancy's coat, wrapping it once around her hand and holding tight as she swished past. Nancy was jerked to an abrupt halt. Her briefcase dropped to the floor. In one movement, she swirled around and yanked hard at her coat with her free hand.

Monica's grasp was unrelenting.

"You black bitch! Let go of my goddamn coat!"

"Black bitch? Well so are you if we were to get technical about it. What the hell is your problem? And where the hell is all this anger coming from? You're acting like a freaking lunatic. If seeing my black face reminds you of your blackness, then that's just too bad. Or is it that you're afraid to be seen with me? You think people might see a family resemblance? Who the hell really cares? You might've fooled a lot of people, but you know and I know, your ass is part black. As far as I'm concerned, you could be purple, but you're still a blood relative."

"Go to hell!"

"You first. I don't even know why I bother; you were never one of my favorite people. That crap you pulled when you were a child didn't wash with me then, and it don't wash with me now. Girl, you had better grow up! You're hurting people that I care about."

Her fists clenched, her shoulders squared and high, Nancy was about to pounce on Monica when she saw the courtroom door open—it was a middle-aged Hispanic woman. Nancy glared at Monica. She hated the woman and the words that she had spoken. Hawking deeply, Nancy spit in Monica's face, the spittle landing on her chin.

Inhaling sharply, Monica could not believe that she had just been spat upon. Unwittingly, she released the coat, reached up to touch her chin, and, thinking better of it, pulled her hand away.

Lowering her voice, Nancy hissed threateningly, "You stay away from me! I'll kill you if you come near me again!" She bent down and snatched up her briefcase from the floor. Plowing through Monica again, Nancy knocked Monica roughly against the bench before running from the courtroom.

"Ladee, you all right?" the woman asked Monica.

Tears welling up in her eyes, Monica said softly, "Oh, I'm fine. Thank you."

Giving Monica a questioning stare for an instant, the woman shrugged her shoulders and left the room.

Just in case the spit slid off her chin, Monica bent forward at the waist so it wouldn't drop onto her blouse. Going over to her pocketbook, she searched the bottom for a tissue—somehow they always ended up underneath everything. Finding one, she wiped frantically at her chin until it tingled.

"I be damned!" Monica said aloud, amazed by the scene that she had just played out with her cousin. "What in the world was that about? The woman must've lost her ever-loving mind."

She turned and looked back at the courtroom door— she was alone. Wearily, she lowered herself into the chair she had sat in earlier. Tears emptied from her eyes, not because she had been spat upon but because of the deep hatred that DeeAnn had for her.

Who was she to think that she could make DeeAnn talk to her? Damn! She must be getting old. There was a time when she would have annihilated that bitch or anyone for even thinking of hitting her, much less spitting in her face. But then, that's what growing up was about, wasn't it, or else everyone would be criminals. Miss Nancy Michaels, however, didn't think twice about pushing her around. One would have thought her life had been threatened. This whole thing was ludicrous and she would be laughing if her hip weren't aching.

She could never tell Uncle Douglas that DeeAnn had changed her name. He could probably accept that she was passing, but changing her name....

Chapter 7

By the time she stopped running, Nancy found herself at the corner of Livingston and Smith streets, a block from the court building. Out of breath, her throat tight, her chest heaving, she tried calming herself by inhaling and exhaling deeply to increase the flow of oxygen to her lungs. Instead, she started coughing uncontrollably. A flash of heat swept across her face. A young black woman holding onto the hand of a little boy gave her a disgusted look—a look that said don't give me your germs—before she stepped a few feet away. Nancy's coughing subsided only after she popped a peppermint into her mouth and sucked on it between coughs. She was in good shape physically; she should not have been so out of breath from running that short distance.

Furtively, Nancy looked back toward Schermerhorn Street several times—Monica had not yet followed her out of the building, unless she had gone the other way. Stepping off the curb with two women crossing

Livingston, Nancy started across the street, then changed her mind, about-faced, and stepped back onto the sidewalk. She could not go back to the office feeling as she did—scared, angry. Construction work on the new Transit Authority building behind her drew the attention of the passersby and the several people waiting at the bus stop. Nancy feigned interest in order to catch her breath and think.

Men and women carrying briefcases—some rushing, some walking casually—shuttled in and out of the doors of the Civil Court building across the street. Others passed her on their way to the Criminal Court building. Praying that she would not see anyone she knew, Nancy backed up to the wooden barricade that surrounded the construction site and, ever careful of her clothes, stood a few inches away. The brilliant white clouds and the strikingly blue sky gave no hint of the rain that had been predicted by the weatherman on the morning news. Gray overcast skies and rain would be welcomed at this moment; people were less likely to give direct eye contact when it was raining and they were carrying umbrellas. Even without umbrellas, most people walked with their heads down in the rain. Opening her pocketbook again, Nancy took out her sunglasses. With them on, she felt less conspicuous.

One of the reasons she had chosen New York as her new home was the indifferent attitude of New Yorkers. This was supposed to be the city where homelessness, drugs, insanity, crime, and dirty streets forced people to wear blinders and develop thick skins and cold hearts. All that she had heard about New York convinced her that she could live here and never be bothered by her past, where her own brother could live in the same block or same building complex and yet never cross her path. Until Monica showed up, New York had been all of that and more.

Meeting Robert had been an extra bonus. He had given her the love she never dreamed that she would have. She ached to speak with him now. She needed to be assured that everything was all right, but calling him on his job was out of the question. Because of the demands of his job and hers, they had long ago agreed to call each other only in an emergency or if their pre-arranged plans changed. Even then, unless they were to meet in a public place, Robert preferred to leave messages that he would be working late on the answering machine at home. To call now would alert him that something was wrong, and he would suspect that it was something deeper than the lie she would have to tell him. He would hate her if he knew the truth. He would never touch her again. Robert was her lover and the only true friend she had, yet she could not tell him her secret.

"Hey lady, you got a quarter?" the raggedly dressed, smutty faced white man asked Nancy. She had watched him make his way from person to person at the bus stop begging for a quarter. While one older black woman had given him some change, the others—three black women, one black man, and one white man—had shooed him away and turned their backs on him. His dirty outstretched hand before her forced Nancy to step back up against the barricade.

"Please lady, it don't have to be a quarter, any change you got will do," he pleaded, stepping in closer.

Nancy held her breath. His body odor was overly pungent. She lifted her pocketbook to her chest and opened it up just enough to ease her hand inside and fumble around for her change purse. She didn't know how much or how many coins she had in her hand when it came out of the purse, but she dropped the coins into the beggar's outstretched hand.

"Thank you, lady; God bless you," he said, going on to his next target, never once checking to see what she had given him.

She had to get off the corner, but she was unable to decide her direction, much less her destination. The B45 bus pulled into the curb and, while a few people boarded, the others were left looking up towards Adams Street for another bus. Checking the bus sign, Nancy saw that four buses stopped at that corner. The B41 bus, which ran along Flatbush Avenue past Park Slope into Flatbush, was the one she could take home, but she didn't want to get on the bus or hail some seedy cab again. She searched the streets for a yellow cab and saw none.

Stepping away from the wooden wall, Nancy guardedly walked back to the corner. Her heart leaped inside her chest—Monica was crossing Schermerhorn Street. Instantly befuddled, Nancy started to cross Smith Street, reversed, and was about to run in the direction of Adams Street when a bus pulled into the curb, its doors opening before it came to a complete stop. Two black women and a middle-aged white man had already stepped to the curb and were walking toward the open door as the bus stopped. Nancy charged for the bus and accidentally bumped the black woman with the little boy in her haste to get to the open door.

"Wait a goddamn minute! Who you think you shovin'?"

"I'm sorry, miss. I didn't mean to shove you," Nancy said quickly, stepping up onto the bus and practically pushing the white man in front of her to move faster.

"You crazy bitch!" the woman shouted from the side-walk, as the door closed in her face, shutting out the rest of her venomous words.

Relieved that the woman did not get on the bus, Nancy sighed deeply. Another unpleasant confrontation with a black woman was the last thing she needed.

The bus pulled smoothly from the curb and crossed Smith Street. Nancy bent down low enough to peer out the side windows to see Monica coming toward the cor-ner she had just fled.

Turning to face the slim, middle-aged white bus dri-ver, Nancy's eyes were drawn to the top of his head. Long strands of sparse brown hair grew two inches above his right ear and swept up across and around the top of his head. Obviously failing at its job of pretend-ing that it was growing out of the crown, the hair let rows of pink skin peek through. To her it was comical that white men vainly attempted to camouflage their lack of hair by letting their hair grow long enough on the sides to practically wrap around their whole heads. To her it looked idiotic.

"Miss, your fare please," the bus driver pleasantly reminded her, giving her a smile.

"I'm sorry," Nancy said.

She swayed with the movement of the bus. Her left arm wrapped snugly around a pole just behind the bus driver's seat, Nancy fingered through the coins in her purse for a token. Finding one, she dropped it into the fare box.

"Thank you, honey."

Choosing to ignore the remark and the bus driver, Nancy, grabbing onto the back of seats as she went along

63

to keep from falling, walked awkwardly, side to side, to the back of the bus. She flopped down into a seat near the rear door just as the bus was pulling into Bond Street. As an afterthought, she glanced up at the sign at the front of the bus. She was on the B41; at least she wouldn't end up on the other side of town in some neighborhood she didn't know. Settling back in her seat, Nancy looked down at her hands. They were shaking.

There was no way that she could face Monica again in court or anywhere. John would have to take her off the case, but she knew that he would not accept just any excuse. Short of dying, there was nothing she could tell him that he would accept. If only she could hide in her bedroom as she had done when she was a child.

As a teenager, she had kept to herself in school and at home. Hidden away in her bedroom, she spent hours fantasizing that she was Sleeping Beauty kissed awake by Prince Charming or that she was Gidget romping on the beach with some tall beautiful blond Adonis. Many of her fantasies centered around the life she wished she had—white parents, a beautiful home, lots of white friends, and Edward, the best looking white boy in high-school French class. But that was not to be. For a long time she wanted to fit in, not only in school but in her own family.

She didn't like feeling like a stepchild, and at times she was a little envious of Winston. He was cuddled and pampered by both Wendy and Douglas. She could hear him squealing with laughter when he and Douglas wrestled. Until Winston was three, he was always underfoot, following her around, always wanting to sit next to her. She would push him away or pinch him, making him cry. Then she would tell Wendy that he had fallen. By the time he was five, he probably disliked her as much as she disliked him. As they grew older, they didn't fight or argue because they were never in each other's company long enough to get in each other's way. What irritated her most about Winston were his eyes. They seemed to sparkle like a freshly poured glass of cold seltzer water except when he looked at her. Then his eyes seemed to dull instantly. Every now and then, if they happened to be in the same room, even for a minute, Winston would give her the saddest, most pitiful look before he would shake his head and look away.

By the time she was fourteen, she was taking her dinner plate into her bedroom. Wendy and Douglas tried for a long time to lure her out of her room to join them, but sitting down with the family had no appeal for her, because she felt no unity with them. She was never nasty to them; she just didn't invite them into her life or stick her nose into theirs. Holidays were difficult because she was made to come out of her room. Other than school, her infrequent shopping trips, doing her few chores, or when she was forced to go somewhere with the family, she wanted no part of mingling with anyone. She sat out in the backyard in the spring and summer only when the family wasn't home, or if they were, when they didn't bother her. Hoping to force her out of her room, Douglas had once taken her television, but that had given her more time to fantasize and read. Two weeks later she came home to find that he had returned the television to its place atop the dresser.

Actually, it was television that had shown her that white people had better lives and more opportunities. There was no contest between *The Brady Bunch* and

Good Times. While the white family of six children, a mother, a successful architect father, and the house-keeper had everything, the poor black family on *Good Times* living in the projects with only three children, a mother, and an unemployed, unskilled father ate lumpy oatmeal for breakfast and meatless dinners. The latter was not a life she would ever choose for herself.

She knew that many black people were living better lives than the Evans family portrayed on *Good Times*, her family included, but the struggle was too great and she didn't want to spend her life concerned about her race first and foremost. That's why she studied as hard as she did. Her grades were excellent because she knew that a degree, along with her white skin, would give her the life she wanted.

Even when she got her first job and every other job that followed, she remained silent—"hi" and "bye" more words than she wanted to say. She felt that no one— black or white—would or could possibly understand her inner conflict. She didn't want to be called "white girl," "red bone," or "traitor" by blacks or "half-breed" or "black" by whites. She understood this early in life and determined that she would live as a white woman when she left home. As it was, outside of the house, in school, she was white, whether people saw her that way or not.

She suspected that Wendy and Douglas knew that she was passing, despite the fact that they never discussed it with her. Then again, it wasn't like she left herself open for discussion on the topic. She knew that her behavior hurt them both, but she couldn't help it; she simply did not want to live with them. Wendy was con-vinced that she was having a severe case of teenagitis, but Douglas knew differently. Many of their late-night conversations in their bedroom were about her, which she listened to from inside the bathroom that separated their two bedrooms.

"Doug, she's a teenager. She'll grow out of her moody standoffish ways."

"No, I don't think she'll grow out of what's ailing her; it's too deep. I was moody myself as a teenager, but nothing like this."

"See, she takes after you."

"No, she don't take after me. I didn't hide from my family. Hell, I'm her daddy and the girl don't talk to me. If kids don't get along with their parents, they at least talk to their siblings. Me and Renee had our battles, but we were friends. DeeAnn don't even talk to Winston. She acts like she hates us."

"She don't hate us."

"How do you know?"

"I just know she don't."

"But how do you know? Did she tell you she didn't? Has she shown you anything to the contrary?"

"Not really. I've tried talking to her about it, but she says she doesn't have anything to say."

"So what else is new? Wendy, what happened to that beautiful, happy baby that clung to me, whose eyes lit up like a Christmas tree when she saw me? I miss that; I want that child back."

When he said that, Douglas had sounded so sad that tears had come to her eyes.

It was a few seconds before Wendy said, "She was a sweet baby wasn't she?"

"So what changed her all of a sudden when she was six? That's when she started being so cranky and didn't want nobody to touch her, especially me."

"Baby, I know, and she won't talk to me about it," Wendy said. "We can give her her space a little while longer; maybe she'll snap out of it."

"Snap out of it? Tell me what *it* is," Douglas had demanded angrily. "We need to take her to a damn psychiatrist. The girl don't have any friends, nobody calls for her, and she don't go nowhere but shopping for clothes when she gots to. That ain't normal for nobody but maybe an old person who ain't got no family or friends left on earth."

"I don't think DeeAnn needs to see a psychiatrist; she talks to me."

"About what?"

"She tells me when she needs something."

"Do you call that talking? I don't. I call that being forced to talk out of need."

"Maybe she's a great thinker or something."

"Get real, Wendy. Great thinker my ass! That girl has a problem and we need to be about taking care of it. If I didn't know better, I'd think she was psychotic or something, the way she holes up in that damn room. I'm gonna ask around tomorrow for a doctor, and when I find one, she's going."

"I don't think she'll go."

"We can make her go."

"I don't think so. DeeAnn's sixteen and stubborn. We can drag her to the doctor, but we can't make her talk or sit still while he psychoanalyzes her."

"Then what the hell are we supposed to do?"

"We just have to wait her out."

"I'm supposed to wait to see if my daughter will ever talk to me again?" Douglas asked, his voice cracking. "I'm supposed to wait to see if she'll ever let me touch her? In a few years she'll be gone, and I know she won't be coming back."

To hear them talk filled her with guilt and shame. At the time, she wanted to go to them and tell them that she was sorry for the way she treated them, but she couldn't. Once back in her bedroom, she had cried, for she knew that something inside her would never let her love Douglas as her father or let him touch her, and she didn't know why.

Chapter 8

As the bus eased away from the curb at Bergen Street, she began preparing to get off—adjusting her trench coat over her arm, pulling her pocketbook strap over her left shoulder. When the bus left Seventh Avenue, her stop, Nancy was still on the bus in her seat. It was just eleven thirty, too early to go home and too early to call the office. She would call in at eleven and report the continuance. The law library was a good place to use as an excuse for her absence from the office this time too. Something had to be done about Monica. Nancy's job as an ADA was important to her, and not being in the office when she was not in court was a serious infraction.

At Grand Army Plaza Nancy got off the bus. For a moment she stood looking up at the majestic gold figures adorning the doorway of the Brooklyn Public Library across the street. Possibly because it was still early yet, only a few people entered through its doors.

Perhaps she should go inside herself—then again, maybe she shouldn't. The hushed stillness within the rooms of the library was not what she needed, she did not want to sit quietly and brood. She'd had enough of that as a child. She needed to walk and think. Turning toward the entrance to Prospect Park, she followed two young white women pushing their wide-eyed toddlers in strollers.

Joggers and bikers ran along the side of the roadway in one direction as the cars, the few that were, passed dangerously close. Inside the park, the vast meadow of grass and lush trees ahead seemed to lift the invisible stifling weight off of her chest, permitting her to breathe easier. Crossing the roadway, Nancy stepped onto the lush, freshly cut grass. The heels of her shoes sank into the soft earth, which held onto them, making her feel like she might step out of them. Placing her briefcase down on the ground and lifting her legs alternately, she reached down, pulled off her taupe pumps, and inspected the heels. She tried shaking free the bits of dirt that clung to the soft leather by knocking the heels together. Most of the dirt came off, but the leather would have to be cleaned later with mink oil to restore the shine. Squatting low to the ground, Nancy laid her briefcase open on the grass and crammed the shoes inside. In her stocking feet, she continued her stroll, the grass feeling like carpet underfoot.

Workday or not, if the sun was thinking about shining, Prospect Park had its visitors, all ages, all races. From dog walkers to joggers to bikers to nature lovers to sunbathers. Not wanting to go too far into the park— muggings and rapes were major assaults in the park, day and night—she sat down on the ground on her trench coat near the two women who had come into the park

71

ahead of her with their toddlers. The eager little boys were on the run the minute their legs hit the ground. The mothers chased them down and brought them back to the strollers. The boys cried and wiggled until they were free again to set off out of their mothers' reach. Her heart ached at the decision she had made not to have children.

She turned away from the little boys and was immediately drawn to a teenage couple twenty feet away. The girl, blonde hair fanned out around her head, lay on her back, and her boyfriend lay atop her grinding his hips obscenely between her open thighs. If it were not for the clothes they wore, she would have thought they were screwing in public for all the world to see. A policeman should come along now and arrest them for lewd and indecent behavior. They appeared to be kissing just as deeply as they were grinding. They were disgusting. Turning, she checked to see if the two young mothers had seen them yet. They hadn't. Others walking past the overly ardent young couple glanced over, looked away quickly, and walked on. All except three black boys in their late teens, wearing the national youth uniform of the day—baggy pants slung low on their behinds, big oversized tee shirts, big, untied high-top sneakers, and baseball caps turned backwards.

The boys stood over the couple egging them on, telling the white boy to "Get that stank stuff, man! Don't be no chump; stop playin around! Whip it out and bone the bitch for real."

The girl pushed the boy off of her and sat up, hastily arranging her clothes. Their faces were flushed. The girl looked fifteen, the boy about eighteen. Flustered, the panting boy jumped to his feet and pulled the girl up off the ground by her arm.

One of the boys pointed at the white boy's crotch. "Damn I don't see no bulge. Whut's up with that?"

"Nothing," another of the boys responded. The three laughed heartily, slapping each other's hands.

The boy pulled the girl in front of him. He looked too afraid to say anything to the boys who taunted him.

"Man, you ain't nothin but a wimp," the taller of the boys said, reaching for the girl. "Let me get to that bitch; I'll show you whut to do with the ho," he said, zipping down his pants.

The girl pulled away from her boyfriend and they both ran hard and fast for the exit. Two of the boys were laughing so hard they fell against each other. Zipping his pants back up, the taller boy called out to the fleeing lovers, "If you need lessons on how to do that ho like a man, give me a call!"

Nancy shook her head. The young lovers were lucky that the boys found them funny and were not turned on by their lust. They were wrong for using the park as their private bedroom.

The boys, still laughing, began walking in the direction of Empire Boulevard, when the boy who had offered to give lessons looked over at Nancy. She returned his stare, clutching her pocketbook closer to her body.

"Hey, man, wait a minute," he said to his friends before detouring and walking toward Nancy.

Nancy sprang to her feet. Without taking her eyes off the approaching teenager, she bent down and quickly retrieved her coat and briefcase. Scanning the park in search of a policeman or men who might help her, she began backing up. No one was nearby. The two women had gathered their babies under their arms and were running for the exit, pulling the empty strollers behind them.

Nancy's legs were shaking too hard to follow them. If he wanted her money, she would give it to him, but she would not let him touch her; she would fight. But it wasn't going to be just him; the other two boys were hurriedly catching up to him.

"Hey, lady," he called, only a few feet away.

At the same time that Nancy screamed, "Stay away from me!" she threw her pocketbook at the fast aproaching teenager. He caught it in midair.

"Whut's up with this? You crazy?" he asked, holding the pocketbook out from his body.

"You have my money, leave me alone. I don't have anything else on me. Just don't touch me. You want my watch? Here!" she shouted, yanking her gold Jules Jurgenson off her wrist and holding it out to him. The other two boys had caught up with him and were smirking at her. "I'm an assistant district attorney. If you touch me, you'll be arrested," she said, hugging her briefcase to her chest, ready to use it to defend herself.

"Damn, man. Take the money and the watch and let's go."

Nancy looked around again and saw a white man entering the park.

"Naw, man...."

"*Help*!" she screamed, frantically waving her free arm. The man didn't appear to hear her; he didn't look her way. She began to gasp deeply.

"Damn, this is wack. Calvin, man, she's buggin' out," one of the boys said.

"Damn, Miss Michaels. Ain't nobody gonna bother you," the boy, Calvin, said, tossing her pocketbook at her feet.

She started to yell for help again when it dawned on

her that the boy Calvin had called her by name. "What did you call me?"

"You Miss Michaels, ain't you?"

"You know me?"

"Yeah. You that prosecutor on my breakin' and enterin' case in criminal court."

It would figure, a criminal.

"Damn, you better chill. Heart attacks are a bitch."

"Then you won't hurt me."

"You know, you're wack," Calvin said.

"What do you want?" Nancy asked, pulling her watch back on.

"Whut you jumpin bad for? I only wanted to talk to you 'bout my case."

"I can't discuss your case with you. Have your attorney call my office," she said, only slightly relieved. He might hurt her anyway for saying that. He didn't move. Seizing the opportunity, Nancy picked up her pocketbook from the ground and started to walk off.

"I only wanna say that I didn't break in nobody's crib. I can't go to jail. My mother'll be by herself if I go to jail."

"Don't beg no white bitch, man," one of the boys said nastily.

"Man, shut up," Calvin said.

Nancy kept walking. Calvin followed her.

"See, Miss Michaels, see, it's just me and my moms, and she sick. She got diabetes and I gotta give her her shots. I gotta be 'round to help her. There ain't nobody else to help her if I go to jail."

"Who's your attorney? Is he with Legal Aid?" she asked without stopping or turning around, concerned only with lessening the distance to the exit.

"Yeah. Alan Goldberg."

"What's your full name?" she asked, stepping off the grass onto the roadway in her stocking feet.

"Calvin James."

Nancy's stride was unbroken. The exit grew closer. The man who entered the park was heading away from her, taking the path along the drive.

"I'll get in touch with Mr. Goldberg and he'll speak with you," she said, forcing herself to speak as calmly as she could.

Suddenly, grabbed by the upper arm from behind, she was forced to stop walking and turn around to face the pleading boy. Snatching her arm free of his grasp, Nancy shrieked, "Don't touch me!"

"Damn! You ain't gotta yell! I just want you to understand. You tryin' to put me away. I can't go to jail. My moms needs me."

Disregarding the urgency in the boy's voice, she said, "You should have thought of that before you did the crime." Stomping off, now more aggravated than afraid, she was within running distance to the exit.

"Man, that white bitch showed you her beehind. She made...."

"Shut up," Calvin said to his buddy. "Miss Michaels, I ain't did nothin'. I'll do anythin' to stay outta jail."

Chapter 9

"Child, I thought I'd heard everything. That woman would've kicked your ass to get away from you. And girl, if Judge DeLeone had caught that action, you both would've been in big trouble—the contempt-of-court kind of trouble," Barbara said, dragging the comb slowly through Monica's wet hair.

"I'm keenly aware of that, thank you. I was praying that no one would come in, and in walks this little Hispanic lady. Thank God it wasn't anybody who knew either one of us," Monica said, wiping away the water that ran from her hair down the side of her face.

"You got that right. What I wouldn't give to be working out of criminal court right now. I'd pay big money to be the court stenographer on your case."

"I bet you would," Monica said, crossing her legs.

"I really would. The dynamics between you and DeeAnn would be greater than the trial itself. Two professional black…. Oh, pardon me—two professional ladies on the verge of a rumble in a court of law would feed the legal gossip vine for years to come."

"I know that too. Still, I can't believe it happened. And Barbara, it happened before I knew it. I never even thought of touching her, and when she spit on me, I was too dumbfounded to respond."

"You had to be to let her get away with that. If it had been me, girl, I would've snatched her tongue out of her mouth and shoved it up her ass so fast she wouldn't know which end to lick a stamp with," Barbara said, emphasizing her point by thrusting upward with her hand.

"You're disgusting," Monica said, grimacing. "Anyway, you say that now, but you don't know what you'll do in any given situation until it happens."

"If you say so. But even if I were stunned for a second, once I recovered, I would have chased her ass down and taken care of business. Where I'm from in Brownsville, we didn't play that crap. If we didn't get you then, we got you later."

"You know, you're acting like she spit on *you*. You're madder than I am."

"I am. This whole thing pisses me off. From what you tell me, this woman's been acting like an idiot all her life and everybody has bent over backwards to be nice to her. Damn right I'm mad. People like that pluck my last nerve, and you were only trying to extend an olive leaf."

"Okay, calm down. I'm all right."

"Sure you are."

"Look, I feel sorry for her."

"If you say so."

"I do, okay?"

"Okay with me; no skin off my nose," Barbara said, continuing to comb Monica's hair.

"That's just the way I feel. When I look back on our early childhood, I can see where I could've been nicer to DeeAnn. It wasn't like I saw much of her, but when I did see her, I gave her a hard time. Don't get me wrong; she was no angel. In fact, she was stuck up and nasty to everybody, but I didn't have to reciprocate her behavior. Apparently when she left Detroit, she naively thought she left her family and problems behind. That's probably why she was so shocked to see me. Imagine, reacting the way she did, she probably would've dropped dead if I had stumbled up on her in the DA's office and called her DeeAnn."

"Yes Lord, and I mean deader than these ends of yours. Do you want me to clip them for you?"

"Do you have time?"

"I have time," Barbara said, glancing over at the red and white kitchen wall clock.

"Great. My clipping shears are right behind you in that drawer on the left."

"I have a good hour, as a matter of fact. I don't have to pick up Kaseem until nine. My mother will feed him," Barbara said, taking the shears from the drawer and turning back to Monica's hair.

"Thanks for coming over and relaxing my hair at such short notice."

"Please, you don't have to thank me."

"Yes I do. I'm not one to take a friend for granted. Anyway, I was gonna do it myself. I couldn't have gone another day with it like this. That comb was losing the battle with my roots and my hair was starting to break."

"I can tell. If you had done it yourself tonight after

the day you had, you would've been bald by midnight."

"I would not have. I could've done it."

"Not in the state you were in when I spoke with you earlier. Girl you were crying and asking 'why,'" Barbara said, leaning over Monica's shoulder to drop the clipped hair into her outstretched hand. "You know why. Your cousin wants to be white. Plain and simple."

"Yeah, I was pretty upset for a minute there, but...."

"A minute or two?"

"Okay, maybe three. Give me a break will you? I know that DeeAnn or 'Nancy Michaels,' as she calls herself, wants to be white. And in a way, she has a right to be categorized as white, bi-racial, or anything she wants. After all, she does look white."

"As to her choosing her race, I think society did that for her when she was born and one of her parents was black."

"I guess you're right. But what I want to know is, why is she so hell bent on discarding the whole family? No one in the family has ever really hurt her, except for maybe me."

"Well she can't exactly pass for white with a family of darkies hanging around."

"Yeah, but I didn't make life any easier for her. The more I perceived that she hated being black and being around the family, the worse I'd treat her. I remember one time when I was about seventeen, I saw her get off the bus downtown Detroit with these white kids from her school. They were standing around talking and I could tell that she was passing. I went up to her and said, 'Hi cousin. How's Uncle Douglas and Aunt Wendy?' She looked like she was about to faint. Her friends were looking at me bug-eyed. I walked off leaving her to explain who I was."

"That was mean. No wonder she hates you."

"I can understand that. I said I wasn't nice to her, and admittedly I did it because I knew that was a way to get to her."

"I wonder what she told them about you."

"Who knows? At the time I didn't care. I wanted to hurt her."

"Well I think she got you back this morning."

"I know that's right."

"There. Your ends are done. They weren't as bad as I thought. Do you want a deep conditioner or a quick one?"

"A quick one for now; I've been conditioning every two weeks. There's some on the second shelf in the hall closet."

"I'll get it," Barbara said, heading out of the kitchen.

Monica examined the bits of hair in her hand before brushing them into a paper towel. Balling the paper up into a tight wad, she tossed it into the garbage container against the wall next to the sink.

"Three points!" Barbara said from the hall. "Wow! How do you find anything in here? I thought you were gonna organize this closet."

"For your information, it is organized in there. That's all right, I'll get it. I know where everything is," she said, getting up quickly and going out into the hall to the narrow, combination linen/toiletry/cosmetic closet outside the bathroom. "It's a good thing the rest of your apartment doesn't look like this closet, you might scare Dayton away."

"If this closet scares Dayton away, then he needs to stay away."

"So cavalier. If that hunk vamoosed, you'd have a stroke."

"Maybe, maybe not. It's not something I worry about."

"Sure, tell me another."

"I don't," she said. "Barbara, you better watch it; you grow more cynical every day."

"That's what my mother said the other day. She said I should've been born in Missouri, the 'Show Me State.'"

"For real."

"Am I that bad?" she asked, feigning surprise.

"As if you didn't know."

"Well, what can you do? I'm too old to change. Anyway, where is our man tonight?"

"Our man is at a community conference."

"Does he know about today?"

"Not yet. I haven't tried to call him; it's a busy day for him."

"Does he know about DeeAnn?"

"I told him about her last week after I saw her downtown."

"He's not gonna like what she did to you."

"I guess not, but there's nothing he can do about it, is there?"

"Maybe not, but he can make you feel better. Oh, I better call my mother and remind her what time I'm coming over. She'll forget that I told her nine and blame me for being forgetful."

"Use the phone in the bedroom; the static is awful on that cheap cordless in the living room."

"So why did you buy cheap? You know you get what you pay for."

"I didn't buy it; I got it as a consolation prize in some

82

promotion sweepstake. I won't enter any more of those."

"I don't waste my time," Barbara said from the bedroom.

She was glad that Barbara had come over to do her hair and engage in her special brand of raw humor—she rarely held her tongue, and her cynicism was growing in leaps and bounds. Most days she took Barbara with a grain of salt. She was a good friend.

After her eventful little meeting with DeeAnn, the rest of the afternoon had been miserably long. When she got home she called Barbara before she even sat down. Luckily for her, she had just walked into her apartment too. The tears had come unbeckoned when she heard Barbara's voice, which is why she hadn't called home first. Renee would have been upset if she had cried over the telephone, especially because of DeeAnn. She felt as strongly as she did about DeeAnn's snubbing the family.

Until Barbara rang the doorbell, Monica had sat on the floor in front of the stereo in the living room half listening to the radio. The harder she tried not to think about DeeAnn, the more she dwelled on her.

"Did you find the conditioner?" Barbara asked, coming back into the hall.

"Of course I did," she said, handing her the blue and white plastic bottle.

"Monica, you look so sad. You're still upset, aren't you? I told you, you better stop worrying about that woman. She'll have you turning gray."

"Please, not yet."

"Oh no. Seems like I saw one or two up there, and you probably got them both today."

"Thanks a lot, smarty," she said, laughing in spite of herself.

"Keep it up; next weekend there'll be ten more. Come on, let me get this stuff on your head."

Going back into the kitchen, she sat while Barbara stood over her pouring the white creamy conditioner on top of her head and then massaging it into her hair and scalp.

"Hmmmmm…, that feels good."

"Want your head covered in plastic?"

"Yes. Use the plastic wrap there under the counter. Is everything okay with your mom?"

"Sure, no problem. Kaseem's fed, his homework's done. My mother's good with algebra. By the time Kaseem's in seventh grade, he'll be good and ready for geometry. See how far ahead of us they are today. I didn't get geometry until the ninth grade."

"Neither did I. But it's great he's in a good school that believes in teaching and not in quotas," she said, admiring Barbara for her determination to raise her son to the best of her ability.

She had been married to Kaseem's father, Alex, until Kaseem was four years old. Alex had walked out after telling Barbara that he loved her but that married life was suffocating him. After they were married, Alex, who had been a private person when they were going together, became even more so, he liked to come and go without question. He spent hours listening to jazz and was reluctant to share himself or his time with Barbara. At times they fought about him living as if he was the only one who counted. They drifted further apart—Barbara grew angrier. Finally, when Alex wanted to leave, she let him. He moved to Atlanta a month later. He visited his son on his birthdays and at Christmas. Every August he took Kaseem for three weeks. The first of every

84

month, Alex sent Barbara a check for four hundred dollars for Kaseem's support, which Barbara was satisfied with, considering they never went to court to decide the amount.

Nine years had passed since the divorce, and it had taken Barbara six of those years to get over the pain of rejection and loss. She and Alex had become friends once she let herself accept the fact that it was nothing she had done wrong, that Alex was really not such a bad guy, and the way he chose to live his life was his problem. He was happiest as a single.

"Your cousin DeeAnn reminds me of a movie my dad told me about a few years ago."

"What's the name of it?"

"I don't recall right off," Barbara said, rinsing her hands. "Something about color. But it was about New Orleans society, I guess around…the 1800s. It seems that it was socially acceptable in the French Quarter for a wealthy white man to take a mixed-race woman and keep her."

"Keep her in his house?"

Sitting down at the table across from Monica, Barbara said, "*Keep* her. Monica, I know you know what I mean. You know, as in 'kept woman.'"

"Oh shoot! Don't mind me, I'm a little slow tonight."

"Anyway, white men set their quadroon mistresses up in apartments or houses and visited them for sex and fun. They even had children together—a second family for the white man. And these women were well kept— nice homes, beautiful clothes, jewelry, whatever. By the way, the lighter the women were, the better, and they could not have ever been touched by a black man."

"So all of these women were mixed?"

"I guess after the first one, sure. The female children were reared to give pleasure to white men, who would literally purchase them by making a financial arrangement with their mothers. The girls were introduced at a Quadroon Ball—something like a debutante ball—which was attended by wealthy white men and the mothers of these girls."

"What happened to the male offspring of these lustful unions?"

"I asked my father the same question. He said there were no male quadroon children portrayed."

"I'm not surprised. Black males were never the white man's favorite species, light skin or not, and those sweet virginal southern belles weren't about to openly keep a stud for their pleasure."

"Not hardly. But the boys were free just like their mamas were. They probably became craftsmen or businessmen."

"Most likely," Monica agreed.

"These girls were schooled, groomed, taught to dance and entertain. The whitest looking girls commanded the highest price and were in great demand. They didn't associate with black people, freed or enslaved, and after a while, either as a gift or as a gesture before the master died, the more fortunate women were left a legacy."

"The word 'fortunate' is relative. Speaking for myself," Monica continued, "I would not have wanted to be in any of their shoes. Whether they chose to slave in the cottonfields or sit in the lap of luxury, they were still slaves, freed or not."

"That's probably why some of them chose not to pass. Everybody didn't take the easy way out."

"No, not everyone," Monica said, patting her plastic-wrapped head. "Then this movie is based on fact?"

"Who knows? You know how they make a movie seem legit when in fact it's fiction. There was a class system in New Orleans amongst blacks. Probably still is to some degree."

"Do you remember a short-lived sitcom on television called *Frank's Place,* with Tim Reid and his wife?"

"Vaguely," Barbara said after thinking for a second.

"Well, it was about a restaurant owner in New Orleans. In one episode, there was the issue of this private black club that wanted Frank to join up, which he was eager to do, by the way. That is, until he found out that the criteria for membership was that a prospective member's complexion could not be darker than a brown paper bag."

"As my grandmother use to say, 'I declare.'"

"I'm telling you. Frank didn't join, he was appalled by the audacity of black people having the nerve to do to their own what white people had being doing all along with their whites-only clubs."

"Good for him. It's a shame they cancel shows that enlighten people."

"Barbara, you and I both know, that's because the majority of people are not supposed to be enlightened; it's too dangerous. So anyway, many of those quadroons must have seen themselves as white. Their sons and daughters were not permitted to marry dark-skinned blacks. Their offspring maintained that brighter or whiter ideal and quite literally disowned anyone who did marry darker than themselves."

"You got that right. And girl, they probably would have killed for a jar of relaxer in those days."

"Oh stop," Monica said, laughing.

"Really. Just think about it. All those girls couldn't have had straight hair. I'm sure some of those heads could've doubled as steel wool," Barbara said, throwing her head back and laughing.

"That's ugly. You're terrible."

"You know it's the truth."

"DeeAnn would've fit nicely in that society. She would've been quite an acquisition for the richest man in town, except she would've been indignant if they called her 'quadroon,' 'negress,' or 'mistress.'"

"I hadn't thought about it, but do you think she has a man, a white man?"

"Let's just say, if she has any man, he's a white man. You'd be putting her in another category if you're suggesting that she'd see a black man, then you're talking interracial. She's running away from that, remember? She wouldn't be caught dead with a black man."

"She can have all the white men she wants, even my share. I like my men darker than sand—way darker," Barbara said, turning on the faucet at the kitchen sink and testing the temperature of the water with her hand. "I'm real glad I don't have her problem."

"I know what you mean. Our plight as black people is tough enough without that added stress. Though interestingly, in college and law school, I knew quite a few mixed-race people, and they all identified themselves as black. There were definitely a few who could pass and didn't opt to do so. They had black friends and white friends. However, I would have loved to have been a fly on the wall when they let on to their white friends that they were mixed-race. White people can't always tell if a person is of color, you know. One girl told me that white people were good at letting down their guard around her because they thought she was one of them. If no noticeably black person was around, white people would talk about blacks, and she'd have to let on that she was black, because she said she always thought about her mother when they talked badly about us."

"That's awful. I wonder if they all let on when they're around white people."

"Well, I never got the impression that the people I knew in school were ashamed of being mixed-race. There was one girl who said that she wished that she was darker so people would stop asking her what she was. She, and others, joined the black sororities and fraternities. It was other people, blacks specifically, who were the problem for them. The sisters sucked their teeth and rolled their eyes when they saw one of these women with a brother, and the brothers looked disgusted if they saw a sister with what they thought was a white man."

"There's a lot of money to be made in tee shirts that say 'Black and Proud of it!' or 'White is Skin deep— Black is to the Bones' or 'What You See Isn't What You Get.'"

"Girl, where do you pull that stuff from?"

"Child, don't ask me. My mouth has its own life. It never asks me anything, though it does get me into a lot of trouble."

"You're crazy."

"That's what I'm told. Ready to rinse?"

"Ready," Monica replied, taking the plastic wrap off of her head.

"Grab the towel."

Taking the towel off the back of her chair, Monica placed it on the dish drain. Bending over the sink, she could feel the coolness of the smooth porcelain through her cotton tee shirt. It was somehow soothing. Within minutes, Barbara was finished.

"Okay? All done," she said, wrapping the towel around Monica's head like a turban and then patting her hands on the towel on Monica's head to dry her hands. "Blow dry?"

"Uh huh. But let it air dry as much as possible by itself first; I don't want it too straight," she said, towel drying her hair and then turning her head side to side to make it air dry faster.

"I don't know why you bother relaxing it at all, it never looks straight."

"That's all right; that's the way I want it. Before it's all over, I'll be wearing locks or a short afro. For now, relaxing makes it more manageable, that's all. How's your hair holding up?"

"I can go another week," Barbara said, running her fingers through her hair.

"Just let me know, okay?"

"You'll know when you see me looking like the bride of Frankenstein."

"You look like that now."

"Thanks, pal."

Chapter 10

She should have listened to her inner voice. It warned her not to call home while she was still upset. Renee was just as angry as Barbara but more critical of her actions.

"Where's dad? I don't want him to hear this."

"In the living room watching T.V. I didn't want to hear what I heard either. I hope you spit back in her face."

"No, I did not."

"What's wrong with you? You let that maniac push you around *and* spit in your face. Cousin or not, you don't stand still for that—unless she had a gun. Did she?"

"What kind of question is that?"

"Don't get smart with me. I want to know if she had a gun."

"No, she didn't," Monica replied, rolling her eyes up to the ceiling. There was no use arguing with Renee. She always had the edge and used it: "I'm your mother."

"Why are you sounding so passive? You never took any garbage from DeeAnn when you were a child. Are you scared of her too?"

"No, I'm not scared of her, and what do you mean by 'too?'"

"Too means in addition to her daddy. If Douglas wasn't so intimidated by that little stuck-up wench, I'd call him up, make him jet his wimpy ass to New York City and beat the hell out of her confused ass. But noooo, he's too scared to upset her."

"Why would Uncle Douglas be afraid to upset DeeAnn?"

"Probably because he was always afraid she'd call him a spade."

Inhaling sharply, Monica said, "Mother, you're terrible."

"It's the truth. She always acted like his blackness would rub off on her if he touched her. I never seen a child behave the way she did. When she started calling them by their first names, Douglas should've put her ass out with the garbage."

"He couldn't do that; she was barely in her teens."

"Let me tell you something. When a child is grown enough to call the shots in the house and call her parents by their first names, then she's old enough to be on her own."

"Well, I did used to think she was disrespectful."

"Damn right she was. He should've beat her ass then, and he needs to beat it now."

"Mother, you can't go around whipping a thirty-year-old behind."

"Maybe not, but I think whipping her ass at this point

might wake her up. It can't get no worse. She hasn't come home to see her folks since she left home eight years ago. What difference would it make?"

Monica closed her eyes and rubbed her forehead. She'd had more than her fill of DeeAnn for one day. "Mother, let's just forget about that woman for now; I don't want to talk about her no more. Besides, I just called to tell you that I saw her. I'm over that little altercation we had."

"You sure have mellowed. It must be that Dayton. Don't let him tame you too much; a real man don't want no lackey. By the way, is there a ring on your finger yet?"

"I'm not a lackey for anyone," Monica responded, sitting up in bed.

"You didn't answer my question. Is there a ring yet?"

"No, there is no ring. I would've told you if there was."

"Watch your tone, young lady," Renee warned.

Shaking her head, Monica chuckled.

"Honey, I don't want to get in your business, but maybe you should hold back your favors until Mr. Dayton comes around. He's a good-looking man and all…."

"I'm not about to start playing games to get a ring on my finger. If it's meant for Dayton and me to get together, we will. Right now, that's the last thing on my mind."

"Maybe it should be the first thing on your mind; you're not getting any younger, you know."

"Thanks for reminding me. Who's paying for this call?"

"Don't get fresh with me, miss; you're not so grown that you can talk any old way to me," Renee said.

Taking the phone from her ear, Monica rested it on her knee for a second before speaking into it again. They always disagreed about her not getting a commitment from Dayton after the first year. Renee didn't believe that a man had to sample the goods any longer than that. At that point, it was show your hand or fold. "I'm sorry, mother," she said, wanting to end the call.

"And, miss, since when do you call me 'mother?'"

"Oh brother. What's wrong with 'mother?'"

"Nothing really. It's just that you used to call me 'mom.' Living in New York City has changed you, hasn't it?"

She wasn't about to argue this one. "If you don't like 'mother,' I'll call you 'mom,' okay?"

"I guess it's all right. It'll take some getting use to. It does sound kinda classy."

"You're a mess."

"Sometimes, but what are you gonna to do about DeeAnn?" she asked, concern clear in her voice.

"I'm not gonna beat her up or anything, if that's what you're asking."

"You probably should."

"Mother, we're not little girls any more. I…."

"Hold on a minute. Stop tapping me on my arm."

In the background Monica could hear her father say, "Well, how long am I supposed to stand here waiting for my turn? I'd like to talk to her too, you know."

"Then you should've answered the phone when I asked you too."

"Why? It's always for you. Just give me the damn phone, woman. You're gonna make me miss my ball game, waiting for you to get finished."

"Just a minute."

94

"I want the phone now. A minute to you is two hours. The damn phone company would go broke in less than a minute if you woke up one morning mute."

Placing her hand over the receiver, Monica laughed aloud. They had a running argument about Renee's endless telephone conversations.

"Man, a person can't even talk to her own daughter in peace. Monica your father wants to talk to you."

"Mom? Don't tell Dad or anyone else about DeeAnn just yet, okay?"

"I don't know why not, but okay. Oh, I'm 'mother,' remember?"

"Pardon me," Monica said, smiling at Renee's ability to always make her smile.

"Hi, baby. How's the New York lawyer doing?" Kevin's mellow voice asked.

"I'm okay. How are you?"

"Just fine. Me and Kev just finished cleaning out the garage. Your mother was having fits again about being afraid to go in there."

"Kevin's there? Let me speak to him when we finish."

"He's not here anymore. He went home to clean up. Said he had a meeting or something to go to. You know how busy he is—like you. I had a time getting him over here as it was."

"Oh, dad, I call every other Sunday. If you want to speak to me any other time, you can call me. I'll pay for it."

"I'm not talking about telephone calls, I talking about visiting."

"I was home Christmas."

"That was some months ago, I'd say."

Renee must have been standing right next to him because, before she could respond, she heard her say, "Kevin, stop giving the girl a hard time. She has a life, you know. If she was coming home all the time, then you'd bother her about that. Ain't I enough company for you?"

"Oh you're more than enough company; you just wear me out," he said, laughing.

"Don't touch me, you horny old man."

"Dad...dad...dad!"

"I'm here. What are you yelling for?"

"You children go ahead and play; I have to go now," Monica said, smiling to herself. It was nice to know that they still enjoyed each other. She should wish for that with whomever she settled down with.

"Not so fast. You just called last week; everything all right?"

"Everything's fine."

"You sure? You need any money?"

"I don't need any money, dad; I'm fine."

"Okay, then we'll talk to you Sunday?"

"Yes, and dad, tell Kevin to call me this weekend. He owes me a call."

"I'll tell him, but you know how he is about telephones; he'd rather talk in person. He's always got that damn answering machine on. I don't know why he wasted his money; he don't return the calls, talking about he forgot. He may as well not know that anybody called. Your mother had to drive over to his house the other day and she ended up waiting forty minutes before he showed up. She was mad as hell."

Though he was no match for Renee, once he got going, Kevin was no slouch on the telephone either.

"Dad, I have to go."

"Okay, baby."

"Bye. Love you both," she said quickly, hanging up the telephone, knowing full well that Renee was more than likely telling Kevin everything she'd said about DeeAnn—start to finish.

Chapter 11

"Would you state your name and address for the record?"

"Brendalynn Lenox, 531B Hancock Street, Brooklyn, New York."

"Were you at home in the early morning hours of Sunday, September 24, 1989?"

"Yes, I was. I was in bed."

"Were you asleep?"

"No, I was watching television."

Standing in front of the witness stand, Nancy paused before asking her next question.

"Miss Lenox, was there an incident or disturbance that may have distracted you this particular morning?"

"Uh huh, there sure was," she answered, shifting in her seat.

"Can you tell the court what happened?"

"There was an argument going on downstairs underneath me in the Madison apartment."

"Do you know what the argument was about?"

"Objection. Calls for speculation," Monica stated.

"Sustained."

"I'll rephrase," Nancy said dryly. "Miss Lenox, did you hear specifically what they were arguing about?"

"They were so loud anybody coulda heard. Charlene and her boyfriend were fighting about Charlene dancing too close to some guy at a party they went to."

"So the boyfriend was upset about the decedent dancing too intimately with someone else. Miss Lenox, I am not asking for your opinion nor am I asking you to speculate. Did the boyfriend say anything that you could hear clearly that indicated how angry he was?"

"I heard him say, 'The next time you dance with another dude like that, I'm gonna kick his ass first and then your ass last.'"

"What did the decedent say to that?"

"She told him that he wasn't gonna put his hands on her and that he didn't own her, and that she'd dance with anybody she wanted to."

"Did the boyfriend respond?"

"Yes he did. He said, 'If you don't believe that I'll kick your ass, do it again and find out.'"

Never once glancing in the direction of the defense table, Nancy began pacing in front of the witness stand. Brendalynn's heavily mascaraed eyes followed her.

"You said Charlene and her boyfriend. How do you know that it was Miss Madison and her boyfriend you heard arguing?"

"Look, I live in an old brownstone, and living in a brownstone is like living in an open house, except there are doors. The walls and floors are not soundproof or smellproof. At any given time, I know what's cooking in the pots in the other two apartments and I can hear the littlest cough. Everything rises to the top floor. Besides, I knew Charlene for eleven years. I know her voice when I hear it, and in the quiet of the morning, I'm positive it was her voice."

"Do you also know her boyfriend?"

"I've met him and I've seen him plenty of times."

"Is he in the courtroom?" Nancy asked, still pacing, which was not her habit. She had not felt this uncomfortable since she prosecuted her first case. Monica's presence at the defense table robbed her of her usual composure.

Pointing to Rufus, Brendalynn said emphatically, "That's the murdering bastard over there. He should be whipped, dipped, and fried in a pot of boiling oil."

"I ain't no murderer!" Rufus shouted, exploding from his chair and knocking it over. "I didn't kill Charlene!"

"Motion to strike!" Monica exclaimed, leaping to her feet while grabbing and clamping down on Rufus' arm to shut him up.

"Sit down Mr. Washington or I will have you handcuffed to your chair for the duration of this trial," Judge DeLeone said, banging his gavel to quiet the voices that erupted in the room when Rufus spoke out.

"Pick up your chair and sit down," Monica ordered.

"But why she gotta say that? I didn't kill…."

"Listen to me," Monica said, shaking Rufus's arm to get his attention; he was staring daggers at Brendalynn Lenox. "You have got to sit down and be quiet. This is a court of law. The judge will handcuff you if you don't behave. Let me do the talking."

Rufus looked at Monica and at the two corrections officers who had come up alongside him. One of the officers had his hand on his gun.

"Pick up the chair," Monica ordered softly.

Having no other choice, with all eyes on him, Rufus hoisted the chair upright and flopped into it. He did not see Judge DeLeone's reproachful glare as he was staring down at the table, his eyes brimming with tears.

"Miss Hall, restrain your client in the future or he will be barred from these proceedings. I will have no dramatics in my courtroom."

"Yes sir." Adjusting her jacket, Monica proceeded, "Your honor, defendant has not been convicted of this crime and defense takes exception to witness' vulgarity."

"Witness will refrain from passing sentence; that is my job. Witness will also watch her language," Judge DeLeone admonished.

Angrily crossing her legs, Brendalynn sucked her teeth and gave Monica a piercing stare.

"Miss Lenox, do you understand?" Judge DeLeone asked.

"Yes sir," she said curtly.

"Mrs. Meyers, strike those last remarks from the record and the jury will disregard that part of the testimony. Miss Michaels, you may proceed."

"Miss Lenox..., was the defendant in Miss Madison's apartment during the early morning hours of Sunday, September 24, 1989?"

"Objection, your honor. Unless witness saw defendant enter decedent's apartment, she cannot say indisputably that he was in the apartment at that time on that date," Monica stated, staring at DeeAnn's back. Not once had their eyes met.

"Sustained," Judge DeLeone acquiesced.

"Miss Lenox, did you see defendant enter the Madison apartment?" Nancy asked measuredly.

"No, I did not, but I know she was arguing with him."

"Move to strike. If witness did not see defendant enter decedent's apartment, she cannot in fact say that he was the individual arguing with decedent," Monica said from her seat.

"So ordered. Miss Michaels, witness is not clairvoyant is she?"

Exasperated, Nancy responded, "Not that I know of, your honor."

"Continue."

"Miss Lenox, was there anything at all that happened that indicated to you that defendant was in the apartment that morning?"

"Yes, there was," Brendalynn practically shouted, uncrossing her legs and sliding forward in her seat and gripping the arms of the chair. "I heard Charlene say, 'Rufus, get out of my house.' She must've said it five or six times before he took the hint and left. He made a lot of noise leaving too."

The quiet of the courtroom was interrupted by low mumbling from the spectators.

"Order," Judge DeLeone demanded, banging his gavel twice.

Nancy waited briefly before she continued. "They were already arguing, Miss Lenox; what do you mean by a lot of noise?"

"At that hour of the night, he slammed the door so hard the whole building shook. That's when I threatened to call the police if they didn't shut up."

"What time was that?"

"One o'clock."

"Did the defendant leave the building?"

"I thought he did, but I heard him knocking on the door five minutes later."

"Move to strike. Unless witness saw defendant knocking at the door, she cannot testify it was in fact the defendant."

"Motion granted."

"Did the decedent let whomever was knocking at the door into the apartment?"

"I guess she did; I heard the door open and close."

"Did you hear another argument?"

"Nooo..., at least I didn't hear anything."

"Did you hear the visitor leave?"

"No. Whoever it was was quiet this time."

"No further questions of this witness," Nancy said, pivoting and returning to her seat. Pretending to review her notes, she hoped that Judge DeLeone and the jurors had not picked up on her nervousness. Even while interrogating the witness, Monica's presence loomed in her mind. She had not spoken to John Margolis about replacing her on the case; too much explanation would have been necessary. She didn't need to complicate or compromise her job any further than she already had. There was another way to get rid of Monica.

As for Rufus Washington, he was guilty and the evidence against him was overwhelming. She would seek a conviction as fast as possible and end this unwanted association with Monica.

"You may proceed, Miss Hall."

Monica realized that testimony by Brendalynn Lenox could prove detrimental to Rufus, if she did not ascertain that he did not return to the apartment the second time. He had long since admitted leaving the apartment at one o'clock, but fervently denied returning. Monica picked up her notes and approached the witness stand. Immediately she was struck by the change in the witness' demeanor. Brendalynn re-crossed her legs, folded her arms high across her chest, and glared at Monica.

She was not intimidated. "Miss Lenox, you testified that you were watching television at one o'clock A.M. How do you know that it was precisely one o'clock?"

"I know because I was watching *It's Showtime at the Apollo*. It comes on at one o'clock on channel four. I never miss *Showtime* if I'm home on Saturday night, and I'm almost always home. I got two children to worry about," Brendalynn explained, her tone brusque.

"I see," Monica said, returning Brendalynn's stare. "For the record, is it 'Miss' or 'Mrs.' Lenox?"

"Your honor, I fail to see the relevance," Nancy interjected.

"The matter is simple: I would like to address the witness correctly," Monica responded, though she knew well that throwing the witness off with a personal question could dispel some of the hostility.

Brendalynn hesitated in answering until Judge DeLeone ordered, "Witness will answer the question."

"Mrs. I'm divorced," she said, her tone softer.

Nancy sighed and looked down again at her notes.

"*Mrs.* Lenox, had you been watching the show a while before you called down for defendant and decedent to be quiet?"

Brendalynn rolled her eyes upwards to the ceiling before answering. "No, the show was just coming on. What I had been watching went off. That's why I told them to shut up. I didn't want them to drown out my program with their fighting. As it was, I had been listening to them going on twenty minutes."

104

Referring to her notes again, Monica moved to the right of the witness stand. "You also testified that someone knocked at decedent's door five minutes after defendant allegedly left the building. Was a name mentioned by decedent or by the individual knocking at the door?"

"I didn't hear a name."

Monica pressed. "Did you hear anything at all?"

"No, I didn't, but it had to be him knocking at the door. The outside doorbell didn't ring."

"Move to strike."

"Mrs. Lenox, do not give your opinion again or you will be held in contempt of court," Judge DeLeone warned. "Jurors, disregard that last remark; it will be stricken from the records."

Brendalynn Lenox glared at Monica.

"Mrs. Lenox, I am told that Charlene was a kind, considerate young lady," Monica said, striving to bring the tension level down a couple of notches. "You and I both want the same thing, to get the person who took her life."

"That animal you're defending took her life."

"This is your last warning. Answer only the questions posed and say nothing more," Judge DeLeone ordered. Turning to the jurors, he said, "Such outbursts by witnesses are to be strictly disregarded and have no bearing on deciding this case. Again, Mrs. Meyers, delete that last remark from the records. You may continue, counselor."

"Thank you, your honor," Monica said. Turning to the witness stand, she asked, "After the knocking at the door and the door opening and closing, did you hear the Madison apartment door open and close again later that morning?"

"Yeah…, no…, I didn't."

"Is it yes or no?"

"I think I heard something, but I'm not sure."

"Thank you. I have no further questions of this witness," Monica said before returning to her seat and glancing over at Nancy Michaels, who was looking down at her legal pad.

"Mrs. Lenox, you may step down," Judge DeLeone said.

Brendalynn Lenox rolled her eyes at Monica as she walked past her and out the courtroom.

"Miss Michaels, you may call your next witness."

"The people call Ina Jean Foster."

A court officer ushered in from the hall a petite, gray-haired lady in her late sixties, snazzily dressed in a turquoise suit and matching hat trimmed in white. Sworn in, Mrs. Foster sat tall in her seat, her back straight, her head held high, ready to be questioned. She placed her black patent leather pocketbook in her lap and neatly folded her hands on top of it.

"State your name for the record please," Nancy instructed.

"My name is Ina Jean Foster."

"Mrs. Foster, do you own the brownstone at 531B Hancock Street?"

"Yes, I do. My husband Chester and I bought that house back in 1954. He passed on six years ago."

"Do you also live at 531B Hancock Street?"

"Yes, I do. I live in the ground-floor apartment."

"What floor did Charlene Madison live on?"

"She and her family live…lived…live on the parlor floor, right above me."

"The parlor floor?"

"The parlor floor is like saying the second floor."

"Did you see or hear anything on Sunday, September 24, 1989, at one o'clock in the morning?"

"Yes, I did. Charlene, bless her sweet little heart, had an awful fight with her boyfriend."

"When you say fight, do you mean a verbal altercation or a physical encounter?"

"I guess it was a verbal altercation. It was loud, 'cause it woke me up. I was pretty upset when I looked at my clock and saw that it was twelve forty-five. I had to get up at eight o'clock in the morning. I go to church every Sunday—I'm a deaconess. I can't be sleepy in church; I think it's terribly rude when people fall asleep in church."

"When you heard the argument upstairs, did you do anything?"

"I was going to go upstairs after a little while, but the arguing stopped and the boy left."

"How do you know that he did in fact leave?"

"When the door upstairs slammed, I hurried to my living room window and peeked out through the blinds. I didn't see who it was until he got down the stairs and passed in front of my window going towards Lewis Avenue."

"It's pretty dark at one in the morning; were you able to see clearly who it was?" Nancy asked.

"There's a streetlight three doors from my house; I could see clearly who it was. It was that boy sitting there," Mrs. Foster said, inclining her head in Rufus' direction.

"Let the record show that witness has indicated defendant. Mrs. Foster, had you ever seen defendant before that night?"

"Of course I have. He came to the house often enough to see Charlene, and I know him to say hello to. He always spoke."

"Did you see defendant come back?"

"No…, but then I went back to bed after he left."

"Did you hear anything else that night?"

"Yes, I did. I was drifting off to sleep when I heard what sounded like feet shuffling on the floor above, and those floors are parquet. Do you know how loud foot-steps sound on a wooden floor at night?"

"I can imagine. What exactly do you mean by shuf-fling?"

"You know, like quick dance steps or more like some-body scuffling or something. It didn't sound like one person either. I was about to get out of my bed and go up there and put my foot down when it suddenly got quiet."

"Mrs. Foster, could you tell in which room this scuf-fling took place?"

"It wasn't directly over my head, it was coming from the living room. I had gone back to my bedroom, two rooms away. To tell you the truth, I was confused when I heard the noise 'cause I know the boy had left. Then I thought that maybe the mother and sister had come home."

"Did you get up again?"

"No, I didn't, and I'm sorry I didn't. Maybe I could've saved that sweet child's life. That boy must've come back after I left the window."

"Move to strike."

"Remove that last remark from the record," Judge DeLeone ordered.

"Mrs. Foster, did you see defendant again that night?"

"No."

"No further questions."

Monica stood up immediately and passed Nancy on her way to the witness stand. "Mrs. Foster, you say that defendant spoke to you. Did he speak to you every time he saw you?"

"Yes, he did."

Softening her tone of voice and standing directly in front of the witness, Monica asked, "Was he pleasant? Was he always mannerly?"

Nodding her head, Mrs. Foster conceded, "Yes, he was."

"Mrs. Foster, have you ever seen Charlene and Rufus together for more than a minute?"

"Several times. I have a barbecue in my backyard for the big-three summer holidays and I invite my tenants. Charlene asked me if she could bring her boyfriend and I let her."

"So you've had ample opportunities to witness defendant's behavior around Charlene. Did you ever get the impression that he abused her in any way or that he easily lost his patience with her?"

"No, I can't say that he ever gave me that impression. Actually, he was quite gentle with her. He didn't seem to have a problem with getting up and getting things for Charlene. You know how most men want their women to serve them; well, that boy there didn't seem to mind. What I recall most about the young man was that he smiled a lot."

Referring to her notes again, Monica asked, "Mrs. Foster, how many doors are there to your brownstone from the street? Specifically the doors at the top of the stairs."

"Two."

"Are both these doors locked at all times?"

"Well, yes."

"Are the locks slam locks or dead bolts?"

"On no, they're not slam locks. Slam locks can be opened with a credit card. I saw that on T.V."

"So both doors have dead bolts?" Monica asked.

"Yes."

"Does that mean that your tenants must personally accompany departing guests to the door and manually turn the tumbler in order to lock the doors behind them?"

Mrs. Foster did not answer; she appeared to be thinking.

"In order to lock the doors behind departing visitors, do your tenants have to manually turn the tumbler?"

"Yes."

"Mrs. Foster, did you hear Miss Madison leave her apartment, and if so, did you hear her lock the doors behind defendant?"

Mrs. Foster shook her head no before she finally said, "No, I never heard Charlene leave the apartment."

"Can we assume then that when the doors are locked, anyone seeking admittance must ring the bell? Is this so?"

"Yes."

"Does the bell ring in the individual apartments?"

"No."

"So there's one bell for three floors?"

"No. I have my own bell, and there's one bell for the other two floors. One ring for the Madison apartment, two rings for the top floor."

"In that case, can you hear the bell for upstairs ring down in your apartment?"

"When it's quiet I can hear it."

"Can we in fact assume that it was quiet after defendant left the building?"

"Yes, it was."

"Did you hear the bell ring?"

"No."

"Then, Mrs. Foster, at one o'clock on the morning of September 24, 1989, we can also assume that the doors were left unlocked after defendant left the building, which in turn permitted entry to someone unseen and unheard and not necessarily the defendant."

"I...I guess."

"Thank you," Monica concluded, returning to her seat.

"The witness may step down," Judge DeLeone instructed. Glancing at his watch, he announced, "Due to the lateness of the hour, we'll adjourn and reconvene nine o'clock tomorrow morning." Striking his gavel once, Judge DeLeone was out of his chair and out of the courtroom posthaste.

Monica didn't see ADA Nancy Michaels snatch her open briefcase off the table and rush out of the courtroom.

Chapter 12

"Welcome back."

"Hey, lady."

"When did you get in?" Monica asked from the doorway of her office of the man sitting at her desk.

"I walked into the office fifteen minutes ago, but I got back in the city around noon. I was just leaving you a note," Alistair Evans said, getting up from the desk. Crumpling the unfinished note up in his hand, he stuffed it inside his jacket pocket.

Going over to her desk, Monica laid her briefcase down. As Mr. Evans stepped around her to let her get to her chair, she noticed that his belly seemed bigger, fuller. In two weeks he must have surely had his fill of good southern cooking.

"How was your trip?"

"Sleepless and long," he said, walking around her desk. "I've been to two states and five cities."

"Have a seat," Monica offered, sitting down herself

behind the desk. "I hope you have something for me. The Rufus Washington case began today, you know."

"I thought it was to start Monday. What happened?"

"For one thing, a new ADA was assigned to the case at the last minute, and frankly I have a problem with the substitute."

"Like what?"

"I wouldn't want to bore a seasoned investigator such as yourself. I just don't like her."

"If you say so," Mr. Evans said, lifting his right leg and resting his ankle on top of his left thigh. Twenty-five years with the New York City Police Department and ten years as an investigator with Legal Aid were not lost on him. When lawyers didn't want to give up information, they didn't. His feelings were not hurt though; he and Monica had a good working relationship. The truth was, he would have asked her out long ago if she had shown the slightest interest.

"Did you find Delroy Brown?"

"I did," Mr. Evans said, smiling at Monica, purposely lowering his eyelids.

"Stop flirting with me."

"Do I have to?"

"Behave yourself or I will tell Lenora that you flirt shamelessly with me," Monica threatened halfheartedly. He flirted with all the women in the office, mostly smiles and compliments, nothing obscene. Interestingly, he had never dated anyone in the office until Lenora.

"Oh, don't do that. Lenora likes you and I wanna keep it that way," he said seriously.

Lenora worked as an administrative assistant to the attorneys in Trial Part 4, and she was jealous of any woman she thought was too friendly with Mr. Evans.

Like many of the secretaries and assistants, Lenora had been with Legal Aid since the early 1970s and, like so many, she had dated her share of attorneys. But Lenora and Mr. Evans were more than a passing fancy. After two years of dating, they were getting married in July, which for him was six years after losing his wife of thirty-three years to breast cancer.

"Then behave," Monica said.

"Okay. On to business then. Delroy 'Flash' Brown is back in New York."

"Great."

Holding up his hand, Mr. Evans said, "Not so fast. We have no access. He's being held by the DA's office at the Brooklyn House of Detention. They got him on an outstanding bench warrant for dealing a small quantity of crack back in '89."

Leaning forward in her chair, Monica asked, "How did that happen? I thought you located him first."

"I did. Brown wasn't home when I tracked him to his cousin's house in Charleston. I staked out the house for nine hours. I left to get some breakfast around seven, and when I got back, the DA's gumshoe had the locals handcuffing him on the front porch."

"Damn!"

"I wasn't too thrilled myself, but look at it this way, he is back in New York. He'll testify for the prosecution, but remember, you suspect him of murder, so he would've been a hostile witness for you anyhow. This way he won't know you suspect him until you get him on cross. Let the DA's office hold his hands. They're probably putting him through his paces as we speak. They got him on other charges but want him as a witness on this case."

"Obviously they want him to testify about his fight with Washington and to corroborate the argument between Madison and Washington before they left the party," Monica said, stretching a rubber band between her fingers. "Do you think they suspect him of this murder?"

"My guess is no. I was extended professional courtesy and given the arrest details. There was no mention of suspicion of murder. However, don't be surprised if they make a deal with him on that drug rap," Mr. Evans said, taking out a pack of cigarettes and lighting one. "It might not be a bad idea if you consulted with the DA's office and let them know that they might be holding the real killer."

"Not a good idea," Monica said, getting up and opening the window near her desk. "This ADA is not open to any suggestions or opinions from me."

"Why not?"

"Trust me, she's not interested," she said, waving her hand to fan away the smoke that drifted toward her.

"Hey, I'm sorry. I keep forgetting about you non smokers," Mr. Evans said, looking around for an ashtray to put his cigarette out in.

"No problem, this time. Puff fast though," Monica said, sitting down again in her chair.

Smothering the lit tip of the cigarette between his thumb and forefinger, he said, "I don't need it anyway. Lenora said that, if I smoked on her wedding day, I wouldn't have a honeymoon worth remembering." The unlit cigarette went into his pocket along with the balled up note.

"Good for her. I wouldn't want smoke breath all over me on my wedding night either."

"Oh?"

"Watch it. I do have Lenora's home number."

"You're always spoiling my fun," he said, withdrawing from his inside breast pocket a fairly worn, brown, leather-covered notebook. Flipping it open, he scanned the page.

"So, were you able to determine where Brown went after the party broke up?"

"Let's see…, After the party, Brown and three of his cohorts drove, in Brown's car, to a social club on Thompkins Avenue. When I got back in town this morning, I caught up with his buddies. All three vouch for Brown."

"How were you able to find all three today?"

"Are you kidding? Boys like that have no life outside of standing on the corner or sitting on the stoop. They don't move too far off the block."

"What a waste."

"Yeah, but whatcha gonna do? Anyway, one of the boys, Daniel Baptiste, slipped up and told me that Brown left them at the club a little before one, forcing them to make it back home to East New York on their own. Believe me, he didn't mean to tell me that."

"I bet he didn't. I'll get someone to serve a subpoena on Baptiste tomorrow morning."

"I got his address right here. Not surprising, however, Baptiste tried to clam up on me. Of course, I persuaded him to keep talking. Seems that Brown said that he was going to see Charlene Madison and didn't want them tagging along. Baptiste says that Brown couldn't stop talking about getting her back."

"Getting her back? Do you mean he used to go with Madison?"

"Seems so. However, Baptiste couldn't say for certain when it was they had gone together. Didn't Washington tell you Brown and Madison were a twosome once?"

"No, he didn't. I wonder if he even knows. I'll have to ascertain whether or not Rufus knew this," Monica said, writing a note to herself. "Rufus told me that the night of the party was the first time he'd ever seen Brown."

"If this is true, even if Brown went to the social club with the boys, he wouldn't have had to follow Madison and Washington to Madison's apartment. He already knew where she lived, which, by the way, was only about seven blocks from the social club. And it would explain why she would've let him into the apartment, being upset with Rufus for fighting and making a scene and all. A friendly face...."

"That's right, and I've already ascertained that the doors to the building itself were unlocked. The question is, why would Brown kill Madison?"

"Maybe she turned him down."

"Could be. The autopsy revealed that she did not have sex before she died."

"You know, I've been thinking about why there were no fingerprints on the doorknobs other than the decedent's mother's and sister's. Even the decedent's prints should have been on them. The killer must've wiped them off. It stands to reason that, if Washington admits to being in the apartment and his prints are not on the main doorknobs, he might not be the killer."

"I agree, but the prosecutor will argue that he wiped them off himself, hopefully thinking that no one would know that it was him arguing with Madison."

117

"Naw, it still don't wash. That would mean that either he would have had to kill her before he left the building at one o'clock, which he didn't because the landlady downstairs heard noises afterwards, or that he came back and killed her and then wiped the doorknobs. He knew that Brendalynn Lenox heard him slam the door. Additionally, why admit to being in the apartment and not admit to wiping off the prints. Unless he's stupid. I can't believe he'd wipe the prints off and still admit to being there, witness or not. That's why I think someone else, perhaps Brown, killed Madison and had the presence of mind afterwards to wipe away any evidence of his being there," Monica concluded.

"I guess my job continues; I have to prove that Brown was in the apartment. Check this, Baptiste practically begged me not to let on to the others that he spilled the beans."

"Too bad. I feel so sorry for him. I need to get his deposition. If Brown is guilty, Baptiste won't have to worry."

"Not about Brown maybe, but he might have to worry about Brown's boys."

"Damn! Where do all these little hoodlums come from?" Monica asked. "Does Brown have an alibi for the period of time after he left the social club? Did he go home?"

Raising his hand again, Mr. Evans said, "Whoa, hold your horses? Brown has no alibi. He lived alone in a hall room in East New York."

"What kind of car does Brown drive?"

"You mean did he drive? He drove a 1976 red Seville with a black vinyl roof."

"You said 'did.' Did something happen to the car?"

"He sold it that same Sunday morning to Baptiste for four hundred dollars."

"Getaway money?"

"Most likely. But he could've driven to South Carolina; it would've been cheaper. Unless the car wasn't in tip-top running condition."

"Did you see the car when you questioned Baptiste?" Monica asked, jotting on a legal pad.

"Sure did."

"And?"

"And the car had a nasty dent on the rear passenger side. Other than that, nothing else was wrong with the body. I asked Baptiste about the dent and he said he was in an accident a few months ago."

"Do you buy that?"

"No. Because he couldn't remember where it happened. A driver always remembers where he had an accident."

"Damn! Why is it we didn't get this information during the earlier part of the investigation months ago?"

"Because we couldn't find Brown, and his buddies weren't talking."

"That's all right, better late than never. Now, if we can just put that car anywhere near the brownstone on the morning of the murder," Monica said. "Then we have a case. Until then, everything is supposition and circumstantial."

"I'm working on that now. You know what they say, 'the city never sleeps.' A lot of time has gone by, but all we need is one person who remembers. Someone had to have seen the car if it was on the block. People have a habit of peeking out their windows from behind drawn drapes and blinds," he explained. "And, if I can find the busybody or the nosy neighbor who couldn't sleep that night, I would have found our eyewitness."

"I'll keep my fingers crossed, but we don't have much time."

"I'm on it," Mr. Evans said, looking at his watch. "Oh shoot! It's almost eight o'clock. I'm supposed to meet Lenora."

"I better get out of here myself; I have to be in court first thing tomorrow morning, and I have to move on that subpoena for Baptiste before he disappears." Monica said, standing up.

Getting to his feet also and stretching, Mr. Evans said, "I'm going your way. Want a lift or is that big man of yours picking you up?"

"No, he isn't. And yes, I'd love a lift; I'm exhausted," she said, picking up her briefcase and pocketbook.

"Let's go. Want me to carry your case?"

"I'm fine, thanks," she said, turning out the light.

"Women's lib, huh?" he asked, pushing the down button for the elevator.

"Don't start with me."

"S'cuse me."

The door slid open and Monica stepped onto the elevator. Mr. Evans started on after her and quickly stepped back, stopping the closing door with his hand. "I forgot my own briefcase worrying about yours. I have to get it; I plan to be on the street by seven tomorrow morning."

"Go ahead. I'll wait out in front of the building for you; I wanna get some air."

"Two minutes," Mr. Evans said, letting go of the door and walking quickly back down the hall.

Stepping out into the cool night air, Monica set her

120

briefcase on the ground at her feet. No one was in sight. It was odd about the air in New York, it either smelled of stale garbage, exhaust, or nothing. Right now the air smelled of nothing. That was what she missed most about home—the smell of the soil and the scent of fresh cut grass on the wind in springtime.

From one end of the street to the other, all the storefronts were closed up; the private college building across the street was the only illuminated space on the block. Behind her, the lobby light was dim by comparison. The spring semester had ended, which explained the lack of activity in front of the college. No one was walking the streets. The engine sounds of an occasional car moving along Court Street interrupted the quiet. The fresh crisp air enticed Monica into yawning. With no one around, she indulged in a full yawn, lifting her arms up high to the blue-black sky, her head back, her mouth open wide, her eyes squeezed shut.

Abruptly, arms, feeling more like a metal vise than flesh and bones, encircled Monica's body—one underneath her outstretched right arm and across her chest and the other over her left shoulder, pinning her arm to her side. At once, her heart raced frantically and all sound ceased.

"If you scream, I'll kill you," a man's voice whispered harshly into Monica's left ear from the darkness behind her.

The scream that should have come out of her mouth was just a choking sound, the yawn had caught in her throat. The phantom's hand brutally clamped down on her mouth before she could regroup and scream. His fingers dug into her cheeks and sent darts of pain into her gums. Her head was forced back against the pit of a hard

121

shoulder. The strong arm around her midriff tightened even more, crushing her into a taut solid body. The attacker began walking toward the curb, pushing her with his body, forcing her to walk ahead of him. She tired pushing back with her own body. The body pushed harder.

She was outraged at being made to feel so helpless. Was this what victims of senseless crimes felt when animals took control of their bodies from them?

"Open the car door, man!" the voice ordered, his breath hot on the side of Monica's face.

Oh God, I'm being abducted. He's going to rape and kill me and dump my naked body in a vacant lot or in some godforsaken spot where I'll never be found. I can't let him get me into a car, she thought, her mind racing. She began thrashing about, trying to free herself from her attacker's iron-like grip. Her mind screamed, "Mr. Evans, where are you?"

The attacker was pushing harder, almost lifting her off the ground. Then she remembered what Kevin taught her when they were kids and they were both taking karate lessons. She stopped struggling and tried to drop to the ground. The arms held her tighter, crushing her ribs. Monica let her legs go limp, pulling her body down out of the crushing arms. Trying to hold her up, the attacker let go of her mouth.

"Get up!" the attacker ordered, struggling to lift Monica off the ground.

"Ahhhhhhhhh! Ahhhhhhh!" Monica screamed, petrified at the thought that her attacker might have a gun.

"Man, come help me!" the attacker called to the man in the car.

Monica yanked herself free and rolled away from

122

grabbing hands and started kicking wildly at her attacker with her legs, landing some powerful blows on his legs with the heels of her pumps.

"Get over here!" the attacker screamed at her.

Monica looked frantically about for another pair of legs. She knew that if there were two of them, she wouldn't have a chance.

"Ahhhhhhhhhhhhhh!"

"What the hell?" she heard Mr. Evans bellow.

"Forget the bitch? Let's go!" a voice called from the street. The attacker dashed for the car and threw himself into the back seat. The car tore down the street towards Court Street, its wheels screeching loudly turning the corner.

Mr. Evans had pulled his .38 but could not get a clear shot off before the attackers escaped in their car. He ran to the curb to see if he could read the rear license plate, but all the lights were out on the car.

"My God, Monica. What the hell happened? Are you all right? Are you hurt?" Mr. Evans asked, rushing back to Monica and helping her up off the ground.

"I…." She sobbed, her face pressed into Mr. Evans' chest. The strong smell of smoke stung her nose.

"What were they after?" he asked, searching the street for other people. "Did they hurt you?"

Pulling away from Mr. Evans' chest, Monica tried to calm herself. "I hurt myself more, rolling and scraping on that goddamn concrete sidewalk," she said, massaging her elbows. Reaching down, she gingerly touched her stinging legs. She could feel the large holes in her stockings and blood on her legs. Straightening up and standing awkwardly, it was then that she realized the heels were gone from both shoes.

"My heels broke off. I paid seventy-two dollars for these pumps. That bastard. I hope I kicked holes in his damn legs."

"Were they trying to rob you?" Mr. Evans asked, holding on to Monica's arm while bending to pick up her pocketbook, his gun still in his hand.

"I don't think so. That's what I thought at first, but he never touched my pocketbook. He was trying to get me into that car. They were gonna abduct me," Monica said incredulously.

"Abduct you? We have to get over to the eight four. Did you get a look at either one of them?" he asked, placing Monica's pocketbook straps over her shoulder and then returning his gun to the holster tucked neatly in the back of his pants.

"Why would anyone want to grab me? I'm a nobody. I have no money. Do you think it was a sex pervert or a murderer?"

"Monica, I don't know what the hell that was about. Right now, we have to get outta here. Come on, my car is just down the street."

"My briefcase," Monica said, fresh tears welling up in her eyes.

"It's over there next to mine. You're shaking. Let me get you into the car first, okay?"

Chapter 13

There is something to be said about the single life and sleeping alone. Dayton had set the alarm clock for six o'clock and its sleep-shattering buzz had startled Monica awake. How he was able to jump straight up out of bed with only four hours sleep was beyond her. She didn't have to get up until seven but Dayton had to be walking out the door by seven.

After locking the door behind him, Monica crawled back into bed. She was still sleepy but, once awakened, it was always difficult for her to fall back into a deep sleep. From under the comfort and protection of the covers, she peeked out at the clock.

It was seven fifteen.

She had walked into the apartment from the police precinct at eleven thirty last night to the ringing of the telephone. It was Dayton. He had been calling since nine o'clock, he said. He wanted to know where she had been. Before she could get the whole story out, he was off the phone and, forty minutes later, he was ringing the door-bell.

He had come prepared to spend the night; he was wearing a suit and was carrying his briefcase. Once he determined that she was all right and gave her the warmest of hugs, he said, "You should've called me from the precinct."

"I was all right. Mr. Evans stayed with me and he brought me home. If I wanted him to tuck me in, he would've done that too. But honest, babe, I'm fine."

"Why didn't you have him bring you to my place?"

"Come on, Dayton, I'm exhausted," she said, adjusting the pillow under her head. "I hadn't planned on going to your place tonight remember? I wanted to go over my notes for the trial."

"I could be wrong, but I figure your plans should've changed after what happened."

"I feel like you're reprimanding me. I was going to call you as soon as I got home, but you beat me to it. What's the problem? Why are you going on so?" she asked, sitting up in bed, irritated by his nagging and the sore, achy feelings in her legs and thighs.

She had chosen not to go to the hospital for her minor scrapes, and as luck would have it, there was nothing in the medicine cabinet strong enough to dull the pain. She settled for a warm bath and crawled into bed with a cup of cinnamon rose herb tea.

"I'm sorry if you feel like I'm reprimanding you, but you should've called me," he said, getting up off the bed, where he had been sitting since he arrived.

Uh oh, the male ego was rearing its ugly head, and she was too tired to do battle with that monster. "You're right; I'm sorry. I should've called you from the precinct, but everything happened so fast, I didn't have time to think."

Sitting back on the bed and taking Monica's hands into his, he said, "No, I'm sorry, babe. I guess I'm upset that I wasn't there to help you."

"Dayton, what happened to me is not your fault. You can't know the exact moment people you care about are in trouble."

"I know. But I hate that you were hurt."

"It could've been worse."

"That's my point. What did the police say?"

"Not much really. Almost from the moment we arrived at the precinct, the police began questioning me non-stop, trying to get me to identify my attackers. Since I never did see their faces, I couldn't. Then they wanted to know if one of my clients was unhappy with my defense efforts, and when I couldn't think of anyone, they ruled the attempted abduction random. Case closed."

"Just like that? Aren't they going to investigate further?"

"They have nothing to go on—no identification, no motive, and no reason to think that it will happen again."

"That's because of the city we live in. Random violence in New York is prevalent. People get killed for a pair of sneakers, a car, or for the money they don't have."

"That's what the police said. They were pretty blunt with me. They said I could've been raped and killed. I'm a criminal defense attorney; I know that what they say is true."

"Thank God none of that happened."

"Amen."

"Does Evans agree with the police?"

"To a degree he does. However, he thinks it odd that I didn't see the car pull up, and he's right. The car didn't happen to drive up; the car had to have been parked there when I came out of the building. The police don't think that's a big deal. However, Mr. Evans is suspicious of that, and the fact that the guy who attacked me came at me from behind and not from the car. It was like he was waiting for me."

"I don't like the sound of this," Dayton said, getting up off the bed again.

"The whole thing gives me the willies."

"And the police don't think you should be concerned?"

"They gave me that spiel about being out at night alone, a woman alone, et cetera, et cetera."

"In light of what happened, you had better heed their warning."

"Mr. Evans was right behind me; I really wasn't alone. Besides, I am not going to be afraid of my own shadow because of some maniacs. I have a life. I have a job."

"That's all well and good, but for a while, if you're not walking out with the rest of the Legal Aid personnel, you had better call me and let me know that you're working late."

"Wait a minute...."

"Monica," Dayton said, standing above her, alongside the bed. "I know you're an independent woman and all, but, for now, this is just the way we have to play it. Please don't fight me on this. As you said, you're a defense attorney and you know enough about crime to realize that, though you may not see any reason for a crime, the perpetrator does."

"Fine. I'll call you if I have to stay late."

"Thank you. And watch your back all other times."

"I will. You satisfied?"

"Not really, but I'll deal with it. You've had some week, haven't you? First that craziness with your cousin, now this."

"I swear. I'm beginning to feel like a storm cloud has settled in over my head."

"I hope it's not as bad as that. Still, be careful."

She must have fallen asleep after that, because she didn't remember Dayton undressing himself and getting into bed, and she was barely awake when he dressed and left for work.

"Ohhhh, I don't wanna go to work," she moaned, burrowing deeper under the covers.

As if to tell her that she did, the telephone rang.

"Hello?"

"Hi babe," Dayton said. "You all right?"

"Hi. I'm fine."

"Are you up?"

"Not yet."

"Are you going in?"

"I have to; the trial…."

"Okay. I'll be in and out of the office all day. If you call, leave a message."

"I will. Baby, don't worry about me; I'll be fine."

"Monica, don't ever tell me not to worry or be concerned about you again. I have to go. I'll see you tonight."

The telephone clicked in her ear and a dial tone followed. Holding the receiver out in front of her, she said, "My, we're making serious noises like we're in love; aren't we, Mr. Hendricks?" Hanging up the telephone, she sat up in bed. It rang again.

"Hello?"

"How you doing?"

"Mr. Evans?"

"Yep. How you feel this morning?"

"Like I should stay in my bed."

"Well you could."

"You know I can't. Judge DeLeone would have a fit."

"Not if he knew what happened."

"No, don't mention this to anyone. I don't want this to get around. I'm going in."

"Why?"

"Because I'm all right."

"Only you would know. Do you want a lift?"

"I can make it on the bus. Thanks. What's that noise? Where are you calling from?"

"I'm in a laundromat on Sumner Avenue, around the corner from Hancock Street."

"On the job already? You're tough."

"Not as tough as you. If you're going into work today, you deserve a medal."

"Not really. I'm not fearless. I just have a job to do."

"Watch yourself today. You have my beeper number; call me if you need me."

"Mr. Evans?"

"Yeah."

"Thank you for looking after me."

"You're one of the good people; it's easy to look after you. I'll touch bases with you later."

"Bye."

Hanging up the telephone, she threw back the covers and flung her legs over the side of the bed. The soreness in her legs and thighs brought the horror of the night before rushing back into her mind. What she should've

130

done was stuck with the karate classes she had begun when she was twelve and dropped out of a year later. At the time, her hairdo and nails were more important than kicking and punching. What did they say about hindsight?

Chapter 14

"Nancy, don't turn away from me," Robert said. "Being angry with me won't change anything."

Turning back to face him, Nancy said softly, "Don't raise your voice at me."

"I'm not raising my voice," he said, tossing several pairs of socks into his suitcase. "You know I have no control over unexpected situations that arise during a merger of this magnitude. I told you before, the Alcoa-Warner merger was one of the firm's largest accounts. Right now, negotiations are at a critical impasse and I have to go to Houston if we are to see this merger to fruition. I know you understand; therefore, I won't even entertain the thought that you have a problem with me going."

"I do understand," she said, sitting down in the maroon club chair near the window. "I know I'm being selfish wanting you to stay here with me, but I need you."

"Is there something wrong?" he asked, pulling neatly folded shirts from the drawer.

"Of course not, but I have an idea. Why don't I go with you?"

"Go with me? Nancy, what are you saying? Aren't you prosecuting a case? I may be gone five or six days. You can't up and leave in the middle of a trial," he said, dropping the shirts into the suitcase. Going over to Nancy, he squatted in front of her.

"I don't know what I was thinking," she said, though she wanted to confide in him that she was afraid her black cousin was a threat to their future.

"Are you having a problem with this case?"

"No. We brought in an important witness yesterday and I interrogated him last night. The case is open and shut."

"Are you sure? You've been kinda jumpy lately."

"No I haven't," she said, getting up out of the chair, forcing Robert to stand up so that she could get around him. "Which suits are you taking? I'll help you finish packing."

Robert stood looking at her for a moment before he said, "I'll get the suits. You can get my brush and toiletries out of the bathroom."

"Sure," she said, leaving the room and returning within minutes. "Where will you be staying?"

"I'll have to call you with that information."

"You don't know where you're staying?"

"Not yet. Reservations were made by one of the senior partner's secretaries. A limo will be picking me up at seven thirty to take us to the airport."

"Us?"

"I'm going along with two of the senior partners; the limo is picking me up first."

"I see."

"I'll call you later this evening and give you the particulars."

"Okay. Oh, I'll call Peter and Ellen and cancel dinner tomorrow evening."

"Don't cancel. Why don't you join them?"

"I'd rather cancel."

"It's up to you," he said, carefully placing a navy blue suit and a brown suit inside his Gucci garment bag.

Nancy sat on the corner of the bed, her hands folded in her lap. She was dressed and ready for work, having gotten up with Robert at five o'clock. Neither one of them spoke while he finished packing. Maybe it was for the best that he would be out of town for a few days while she solved her Monica problem. She had been awake all night worrying about whether or not Monica had been snatched. There was a part of her that wanted it to happen, yet there was a part of her that was appalled that she had foolishly put a crime into motion. The consequences would be staggering if her involvement were ever brought to light. She could not believe that she allied herself with a black man, an alleged burglar that she was prosecuting. It was insane.

The squeal of the bell pierced their silence. Robert hurried to the living room window and called down to the driver, "Five minutes!"

"Nancy, do you have a plastic bag for my shoes?" he asked, rushing back into the room.

"Yes, in the kitchen. I'll get it."

Returning with the bag, she handed it to Robert and stood aside while he wrapped his shoes, got into his suit jacket, snapped his suitcase shut, and collected his garment bag and carry-on.

"I'll call you later," he said, brushing her mouth with his lips before rushing out of the apartment.

Locking the apartment door, Nancy went back into the bedroom. She didn't need to look out the front window. She didn't want to see the only person she loved drive away. Robert and her life with him were the primary reasons she was so terrified of Monica. Losing her job would be unfortunate, but another legal position could be secured elsewhere. After all, it was no crime to change your name or claim a race. Another man like Robert, however, might not come along again in a lifetime. Which is why she had called Calvin James.

On Monday in the park, she had asked for his phone number, even then thinking of the possibilities. The very nature of her alliance with Calvin James sickened her. It was his kind that she strived to put behind bars. Yet the irony was not lost on her that it would be his kind that she would ask to eliminate her problem. Tuesday evening she had met with him in the darkness of the movie theater on Flatbush Avenue. It was the only place she could think of that was public yet private, dark and probably empty on a weekday evening. The movie started at eight o'clock and Calvin James was to meet her at seven fifty so that they could enter the theater with the rest of the moviegoers. He was not there at the agreed upon time, nor was he in the theater when she took her seat.

She was grateful that the temperature had dropped into the fifties from the day's high of eighty degrees. The night chill gave her the perfect cover-up for her clandestine meeting—a heavy black, hooded sweatshirt, matching sweatpants, and sneakers. Sitting in the dark against the far wall, waiting for Calvin James with the hood of the sweatshirt pulled down low over her fore-head did nothing for her nerves; she felt overly con-spicuous. She slumped down in her seat and crossed her legs. The movie started, but she had no idea who or what was on the screen. The subdivided theater was long and narrow, and on a Tuesday night, fewer than fifteen peo-ple filled its seats. No one sat within twenty rows of her.

For the tenth time, she strained to look at her watch. Just as many times, she had looked back at the door. The longer she waited, the more she was filled with fore-boding.

This definitely wasn't a good idea, she decided, just as Calvin James plopped down in the seat next to her. She shifted her body to the far side of her seat.

"Whut's up?"

"You're late," Nancy whispered sharply, folding her arms across her chest and tucking her hands underneath her armpits to still their shaking.

"Chill, lady. Don't sweat the small stuff. Anyhow, I ain't that late."

"Lower your voice."

"Damn. This gonna be…."

"Will you please shut up?"

"Man, I ain't gotta take this crap. You ain't gotta dis-respect me like that."

"Look, I made a mistake. I'm sorry for having you come here for nothing," Nancy said, standing up. This was more than a bad idea, this was crazy.

"Hold up a minute," Calvin James said, getting up and blocking Nancy from squeezing past him. "You called me. You said if I helped you take care of your problem, I wouldn't have to go to jail."

His voice, apparently not especially loud since no one

had shushed him, sounded like a roar to Nancy's ears.

"Would you please lower your voice? I changed my mind. You can't help me after all."

"It's like that, huh? Just like that you changed your mind?" Calvin James said, his voice lower but angry.

"Let me by."

"Whut about me? I still don't wanna go to jail. You said...." his voice was getting louder.

"Sit down," Nancy ordered curtly, sitting back down herself.

"Please, Miss Michaels...."

"Don't say my name."

"Sorry. Look, I can do whutever you need doin'. Just give me a chance," he begged, sitting on the edge of his seat facing her.

Although every warning bell sounded in her head, she decided to plunge ahead with her plan. "Okay. I want you to snatch someone."

Throwing up his hands as if they had touched something hot, Calvin James said, "I thought you wanted me to steal somethin' for you. I ain't never killed nobody."

"Shut up. I didn't say anything like that. I simply want you to snatch someone and hold that person for a week."

"Wow. That's deep."

"Forget it," she said, jumping to her feet. She must've been out of her mind to even think about plotting such a crime. Scanning the theater to see if anyone was looking at them—no one was—she again tried to get past Calvin James.

"Man, just wait a minute," he said, pulling Nancy back down into her seat by the arm.

Nancy snatched her arm free of his grasp.

"Hey, I forgot. You don't like to be touched. But look,

I can do it. I can. Who do you want me to snatch?" he asked eagerly.

Sheepishly glancing at him, Nancy said nothing. She had to make herself look at him. It was not easy to look steadily into his face—that is, what she could see of it in the dark—without looking away or lowering her eyes. All of her life it had been difficult for her to look a black man directly in the eyes. She looked away.

"First, do you know of a place you can hold this person for a week without detection?"

"Huh?"

"Where can you hide someone without anyone knowing that she's there?"

"It's a she?"

"The place. Do you know of a place?"

"Yeah, I think I got a place in...."

"I don't need to or want to know where this place is. I want you to be certain that you have a place before Wednesday night."

"No problem."

"I don't want you to harm this person in any way. I just want you to hold her for a week. I want you to keep her blindfolded. I want her scared, but don't touch her. You can threaten to harm her, but don't."

"I don't get this. Don't hurt her, just scare her. Whut for?"

"You don't need to know the whys of this, just do it my way. Don't let her know who you are or where she is."

"Then whut?"

"I'll call you to let you know when and where to release her."

"Whut about food? I ain't got no grocery store."

"I'll give you money to take care of that and to take care of your expenses. You'll need only provide her with water and jelly sandwiches for all I care."

"That's cold. I ain't never been in nothin' like this before. I can get in a jam and…."

"If you don't think you can handle this, that's all right."

"I didn't say I couldn't handle it."

"If you commit, I should warn you that you should never tell anyone about this."

"I gotta tell my main man, Reid. He gotta watch my back."

"Involving another person is too risky."

"He can be trusted."

"I don't think…."

"I need him to drive the car when I snatch the lady. Whut I'm supposed to do, walk her to the bus stop? Who is it anyhow?"

"It's an attorney. She'll be in criminal court on Wednesday, in Jury Six on the fifth floor. You'll have to come and observe her so you'll know what she looks like."

"This is deep. What you snatching her for? Oh I got it. You icing the competition."

"Again, you don't need to know my motives. Either you can do it or you can't."

"Damn. I just axed a question. You can get in big time trouble for this yourself, you know."

"So can you. If you keep your mouth shut, we both will be fine. Here is the time and room you have to go to. You don't need to be there more than ten minutes. She works out of the Legal Aid office. You know where that is, don't you? If the opportunity presents itself, you

139

should either grab her there or follow her and wait for the right moment. She's on a trial now, so it's highly likely that she'll work late Wednesday night. Try to do it Wednesday night. If not, try and grab her by the latest Thursday night. Above all else, you must not be seen taking her."

"You really think I'm stupid, don't you?"

Nancy ignored the question.

"Boy, would I like to know whut she did to you."

"I'll call you Thursday morning. Be at that number you gave me at eight o'clock. You'll get one thousand dollars to cover expenses when you have her in hand and another two thousand when she's released."

"All right!"

"I'll be in touch," Nancy said, starting to get up out of her seat.

"Hold up. You gonna dismiss my case, ain't you?"

"It's not as simple as that. I can't dismiss your case out of the blue. Don't worry about it, you won't do any time."

"I'm holding you to it."

Sticking her tongue into her left cheek and then shaking her head, Nancy stood and said, "I have to leave now. Please wait ten minutes before you get up. We don't need to draw attention to ourselves." Squeezing past Calvin James, she cringed when she touched his knees.

He didn't bother to get up or make it easier for her to get by.

"You gonna give me back the money I spent to get in here?"

"What?"

"You wanted me to come here. I ain't got money like that."

"I'll reimburse you when you do the job," she said, heading for the door.

"Good-bye to you too."

She walked quickly out of the theater with her head down. Once outside, she walked quickly to the corner and took off running down Seventh Avenue, praying that Calvin James waited the ten minutes. She didn't want him to see which direction she had gone. Her lungs seemed to want to burst, but she didn't stop running until she got inside her apartment seven blocks away. It bothered her that she evidently had the common soul of the criminals she prosecuted. But she was fighting for her life, and one's life was either worth fighting for or was worthless. If her plan worked, Monica would be scared out of her mind to the point of packing up and fleeing New York City. At the very least, the case would be postponed indefinitely or another attorney appointed.

Wednesday morning Calvin had been sitting in the courtroom observing Monica. Nancy had not seen him arrive and had not seen him leave. At one point, before the trial began, she almost changed her mind. She couldn't believe that she had stooped so low, but once she saw Monica, she knew she had to go ahead. After all, it was because of Monica that she was forced to resort to such a drastic measure and deal with the likes of Calvin James.

All night she had worried and wondered if everything had gone all right. After Robert left, Nancy took a folded piece of paper from her wallet. Studying the number briefly, she picked up the telephone receiver and dialed.

Chapter 15

Alone in the empty courtroom, Nancy had been try-ing for the past twenty minutes to review Irv Weinstein's notes on witnesses and evidence. Her concentration was weak. In a few minutes the courtroom would swell with people, one of whom would be Monica. Calvin James' failed attempt at abducting her was a double-edged sword of sorts. While Monica's appearance in court threatened Nancy's emotional, personal, and professional security, it was for the best that Calvin James had failed. She still wanted Monica out of her way, but involving herself in a crime to accomplish that end was insane.

When Calvin James said that he would try again, she acknowledged that the opportunity had passed and that, if Monica was smart, and she was, she would not be caught off guard alone a second time. If the attempted abduction had been successful, Nancy might have played out her hand. Since it hadn't been, she had to retreat and rethink her strategy for avoiding exposure. She had panicked and acted out of haste, giving no consideration to what would happen if Monica were accidentally killed or if Calvin James got caught himself and named her. This is why she rejected his request to try again. He was disappointed, which proved his poor moral character. Before he would get off the telephone, she had to assure him repeatedly that he would not do any time on his burglary charge. She planned to meet with his attorney and offer a plea bargain—three years probation.

From the corner of her eye she glimpsed Monica sitting down at the defense table. Her heart leaped in her chest. Her mouth dried. People were beginning to file into the courtroom. Nancy busied herself by pretending to go over her notes.

Monica glanced over at Nancy just as Nancy was shifting her body sideways in her seat so that her back was to the defense table.

"I got the message," she said loud enough for Nancy to hear. On the table was a notice of witness appearance for Delroy Brown from the DA's office.

"That didn't take but a minute," Monica said.

Rufus Washington was escorted in and seated at the table.

"All rise. This court is now in session. The Honorable Dominic DeLeone presiding."

"Miss Michaels, you may call your next witness," Judge DeLeone said, once he was seated.

"The people call Delroy Brown."

Monica groaned. She had hoped that Brown would not be called until Mr. Evans had completed his investigation. Jotting quickly on a legal pad, she asked Rufus if he knew that Charlene and Brown had gone together. He wrote back, "Not until after the party."

Escorted into the courtroom in handcuffs, Delroy Brown was taken to the witness stand, where he was uncuffed by the corrections officer, who then stood back against the wall.

At least six feet tall, Delroy Brown was weed thin. Although he was twenty-six, he was lanky like a thirteen-year-old boy who had suddenly grown four inches in a week—no chest, no butt, a sunken stomach. His oversized shirt was tucked in folds into his beltless brown slacks, which encircled his tiny waist and hung loosely from his body, touching nowhere. Why his pants didn't fall down was one of those unknowns.

Nancy knew that the credibility of her witness was questionable since he himself was a criminal. His testimony and what impression he made upon the jury was important. Then again, she didn't much care. This really wasn't her case. In fact, she felt like a substitute teacher or a pinch hitter at a ball game. Margolis had said that it was an open-and-shut case. Even if Monica won, it wouldn't faze her in the least—as long as their association was ended.

"Do you swear to tell the whole truth and nothing but the truth?" the court clerk asked.

"I always tell the truth," Brown said cockily.

"'I do' would have sufficed, Mr. Brown," Judge DeLeone said. "Be seated. Miss Michaels, your witness."

"Mr. Brown, would you please state your full name for the court and your current address," Nancy instructed, getting up from her chair and going toward the witness stand.

"Delroy William Brown. But everybody calls me 'Flash' cause I deals the cards fast and slick," he said, smiling broadly.

Nancy rolled her eyes up toward the ceiling. "Your current address?"

"For the moment I resides at the Brooklyn House of Detention."

"Mr. Brown, on Saturday, September 23, 1989, there was a house party at the home of Letesha Baily; did you attend that party?"

"Yeah."

"Was there an incident at that party that stands out in your mind?"

"Yeah. I wus mindin' my own business, dancin' with my old girlfriend, Charlene Madison, when that dude ambushed me," he accused, pointing at Rufus Washington, who didn't flinch.

"Let the record show that witness pointed to defendant, Rufus Washington. Mr. Brown, tell the court what you mean by 'ambushed.'"

"He...."

"Defendant?"

"Yeah, defendant. Defendant came up behind me and pulled me away from Charlene. It ain't like we wus doin' somethin in the dark by ourselves. We wus dancin' in a room full of people."

"What happened after defendant pulled you and Miss Madison apart?"

"Whut you think happened? We rumbled. Man put his hands on me, punched me in ma face."

"You fought?"

"That's what I said."

"Mr. Brown, did defendant strike you first?"

"I said he punched me in ma face."

"Did you know the defendant before the night of Saturday, September 23, 1989?"

145

"Nope."

"Had you ever seen him in the neighborhood?"

"Naw, I don't hang in Bed-Stuy no mo. Nothin' happenin' over there."

"What did Miss Madison do when defendant interrupted your dance?"

"She wus tryin to explain who I wus, and when we starts rumblin', she tried to break us up."

"So defendant didn't know you, and he didn't know that you and Miss Madison were old friends?"

"Nope."

"Did defendant stop fighting when decedent asked him to?"

"Nope. Not only didn't the boy not stop, but one time I saw him backhand Charlene to get her offa him."

"That's a lie," Rufus urgently whispered to Monica.

"Shhhh!" Monica urged, while glancing up at Judge DeLeone to see if he had heard Rufus. If he did, he didn't indicate it.

"Man, I mean like *bam*!" Brown exclaimed, slamming his hand down on the arm of the heavy wooden chair. "She hit the flo' like a fifty-pound bag of Idahos. I wanted to help her, but I wus busy defendin maself. You should've seen him. Boy wus wild, nobody could control him."

"Motion to strike. Witness has drawn a conclusion that is beyond his purview," Monica argued.

Nancy glanced impatiently at Judge DeLeone.

"I agree."

Flipping a sheet of paper on her notepad, Nancy stared down at her notes.

"Strike that last statement. The jury will disregard it," Judge DeLeone stipulated. "Proceed, counselor."

"Mr. Brown, you said that Miss Madison was your old girlfriend. How long ago?"

"'Bout four years ago."

"How long did the two of you see each other?"

"'Bout a year."

"Were you intimate?"

"Objection. The decedent's past sexual involvement with witness is irrelevant and has no bearing on the crime perpetrated against her," Monica argued, although she realized that she had spoken too soon.

"Your honor, witness testified that he was once a boyfriend of decedent which gives me the right to establish the depth of their relationship."

"I'll allow the question."

Monica shrugged her shoulders and sat down, thankful for the ruling. This information might work in Rufus' favor if evidence against Brown should mount.

"Were you and Miss Madison lovers?"

"You know it. We wus real good together too. Charlene couldn't get enough of me," he boasted, looking over at Rufus, who was looking down at the table.

"Did defendant's uncontrollable jealousy over your dancing intimately with Miss Madison spark this brutal fight?"

"Objection." Monica retorted, again leaping to her feet. "Prosecution is asking witness to give testimony as to defendant's emotional state of mind. Witness is not a psychiatrist."

"Your honor, if defense was paying attention, she would have heard that defendant started the fight over an innocent dance between decedent and witness, who happened to be a past lover. Jealousy was the motive for the fight and the murder," Nancy insisted.

"I am offended by prosecutor's insulting remark about my paying attention, and it appears that she has convicted defendant based on witness' testimony. She is giving her closing statement before this trial has reached the midpoint."

"Your honor, jealousy is a strong…."

"That's enough," Judge DeLeone said, banging his gavel. "Both counselors approach the bench."

Standing an arm's length from each other, Nancy stared up at Judge DeLeone, while Monica stared at her.

"I will not tolerate cat fighting between attorneys in my courtroom. Make no mistake, I will not hesitate to hold either one of you or both of you in contempt of court. Miss Michaels, you will refrain from making your closing statement while questioning witnesses, and Miss Hall, calm down. Your client will not be cheated of justice. Miss Michaels, continue your interrogation without seeking opinions."

"Yes sir," Nancy said coolly.

Monica returned to her seat, peeved that she was letting DeeAnn irritate her.

"Mr. Brown, what happened after the fight?"

"We wus kicked outta the party."

"Did you and defendant continue to fight outside the house?"

"Naw man. Me and my partners got outta there. We went to a joint and shot some pool 'til two in the mornin'."

Monica made note of the time.

"Did you see defendant and Miss Madison after the party?"

"Yeah, I saw them. They wus outside."

"What were they doing, if anything?"

"They wus fightin'."

"How do you mean fighting? Were they hitting, punching…?"

"Naw, they wusn't doing nothin like that, though Rufus did grab Charlene's arm a couple of times. But mostly they wus arguin."

"Arguing about what?"

"Objection. Prosecutor is asking witness to testify to hearsay."

"Your honor, witness was present and can testify to what he heard."

"Overruled."

"Mr. Brown, what were they saying to each other?"

"My man Rufus there said that me and Charlene looked more like we wus tryin to do the nasty than dancin'. Charlene kept tellin him that I was a old friend and that we wus dancin like everybody else, and that if he couldn't handle that she had men friends too, then maybe they should call it quits."

"What did defendant say to that?"

"He said if he ever caught her dancin with a dude like that again, he wus gonna break her neck, and he did."

"Motion to strike!" Monica exclaimed, again leaping to her feet, while firmly pressing down on Rufus' shoulder to keep him from exploding from his chair. Before the session began, she had sternly warned him against speaking out in court. "Witness is acting as judge and jury," she said. Sitting down again, she winced from the pinching of the scabs on her legs under her nylon stockings.

"I agree," Judge DeLeone said. "The jurors will disregard that last statement and it will be stricken from the record. Miss Michaels, have you any further questions of this witness?"

"I do, your honor. Mr. Brown did defendant say anything else to you that night?"

"Yeah," Brown said, raising his voice and looking over at the jurors. "Just before I drove off, that punk...."

"Your honor...," Monica said, somewhat annoyed.

"Witness will not use that word or any other derogatory words in my court, is that understood?"

"Yeah, man," he smirked, tilting his head to one side but looking straight ahead.

"And you will address me as 'your honor' or simply say 'yes sir.'"

"Yesss sir."

For a second, Judge DeLeone stared down at Delroy Brown. The stare was not returned.

Nancy waited for Judge DeLeone's nod before she proceeded. "What is it that defendant said to you before you drove off?"

"He yelled at me that he'd kill me if I went near Charlene again. That's the reason I left town."

A low murmur rose throughout the courtroom. Rufus' mother said behind Monica, "He's lying."

Rufus, his teeth and jaws clenched, covered his face with his hands. Under the table, both his legs were shaking vigorously. Monica already knew that Rufus was capable of seriously hurting Brown, but killing him was doubtful.

Judge DeLeone cut his eyes over at Rufus. He seemed to be waiting for Rufus to speak out or act up. He didn't. Tapping his gavel once to quiet the observers, Judge DeLeone deferred to Nancy.

"The fact that you were brought into this courtroom by an officer tells us that you yourself are accused of a crime. Would you tell the court why you are incarcerated?"

"It ain't for murder."

"Just answer the question, Mr. Brown," Nancy instructed.

"Yeah, you know. I wus busted for sellin crack. But see, I wusn't sellin it, I just bought it for maself. It wus for my own personal use. I only had four vials on me."

Looking at DeeAnn's back, Monica wondered if it were possible that she really believed that lie. To be fair, it was more likely a half truth. As thin as he was, Brown could be a user. But he was also a seller for a small-time neighborhood dealer. Probably took his payments in crack.

"No further questions," Nancy concluded, returning to her seat.

"Miss Hall."

Quickly flipping through her notes, Monica didn't look up or respond.

"Miss Hall?"

"Your honor," she said, standing. "I do not wish to question witness at this time. However, I do reserve the right to recall at a later date."

"Granted. At this juncture, a ten-minute recess is in order," Judge DeLeone stated, banging his gavel once and then quickly disappearing behind his chamber door.

Chapter 16

"Miss Hall, how come you ain't gonna question him? He's lyin. I ain't never hit Charlene. I never told that fool that I wus gonna kill him. And I never told Charlene that I wus gonna break her neck."

"The timing has to be right. I do plan to question Brown, just not yet. I'm waiting for some important information that will hopefully support your accusation and discredit his statements."

"Whut information?"

"Would you give us a few minutes please?" she said to the officer who had come for Rufus. "Thanks. Rufus, give me a chance to gather all the evidence before I speak, okay? I want to be absolutely certain of my facts before I get your hopes up, and before I stand before the court. You have to trust me."

Looking over at Brown, who puckered his lips and kissed at him as he was led away in handcuffs, Rufus said angrily, "See whut he did. I know he killed Charlene."

"You have to ignore him. If he did it, we'll get him."

"When?"

"Listen to me. If we bring Brown up on charges now without irrefutable proof, we'll lose. Our task is to first clear you. I told you before, give it some time. What's important now is: precisely when did you learn that Charlene had gone with Brown?" she asked, flipping to a clean page of her legal pad.

"Outside after the fight. That part wus true. On the way to Charlene's apartment, she told me that they'd gone together for about a year when she wus seventeen. She said she broke up with him 'cause he was dealin' crack and wus tryin to turn her on to usin' with him."

"How did you feel about that?"

"It pissed me off."

"Why? You didn't know Charlene then, did you?"

"No, but it pissed me off that she knew that he wus a lowlife and she wus dirty dancin' with him. His thigh was in between her thighs and they wus deep grindin'. A woman shouldn't dance with nobody but her man like that."

"Yes, it can get pretty hot," Monica agreed, remembering how every time she and Dayton danced like that, they ended up in bed.

"Charlene didn't see anythin wrong with dancin like that with scum. That made me wonder about her. Plus she was dissin me in front of everybody."

"Dissing? You mean disrespecting you?"

"Yes."

"So you argued about Brown and her disrespecting you all the way back to the apartment and even after you were in the apartment?"

"Yeah, but I didn't kill her. I wus mad at her, but I

153

didn't kill her. I left like I said, but I wish I didn't. Charlene'd be alive today if I had stayed there."

"You can't blame yourself for Charlene's death."

"I do."

"Did you plan on calling her or seeing her the next day?"

"When I left I was pretty mad. And when I went to bed, I told maself that I wouldn't call or see her until she apologized to me."

"That's understandable. Look, go with the officer. Perhaps you have to use the men's room or want some water?"

"Okay."

"See you in a few minutes," she said to Rufus as he was led away. It was true; she had postponed questioning Brown because she didn't want Brown to know that she suspected him. In jail or out, word of mouth and the telephone was almost like being there if Brown had to get to Baptiste and silence him. Until she had more to go on, she didn't want Brown tampering with Baptiste's memory before he could be brought before the court.

Looking over at DeeAnn, she decided that she really did need to speak to her as the prosecutor. The likelihood that Brown could walk on his charge of possession for cooperating with the DA's office on this matter, was highly probable.

"Miss Hall?"

"Yes?" Monica responded, turning around in her seat to face Rufus Washington's mother.

"Rufus ain't never been no liar. He ain't no saint, but he ain't never been no liar."

"Well, that's good to know, because telling the truth is what's gonna pay off for him. Don't worry, he'll come

154

through this, a little scarred but maybe a better man."

"I pray that he will."

"Will you excuse me; I need to speak to the prosecutor," Monica said, getting up from her seat. "Miss Michaels, I need to speak with you about some vital information my investigator has uncovered."

Nancy said nothing. She didn't even bother to look up from her notes, though her brow knitted tightly and her hands began to shake.

Bending and leaning in closer to her, Monica whispered, "Dee..., excuse me, Miss Michaels. I need to speak to you about this case. You're supposed to be a professional. Act like one and put your personal feelings where they belong, outside of this courtroom. If you can't handle it, then I will lodge a complaint with the DA's office."

"Miss Hall," Nancy began stiffly, still not looking up, her throat suddenly so dry that she could barely speak. "There is nothing about this case or anything else in this world that I wish to discuss with you. You are defense, I am prosecution. We're on opposite sides of the fence and need not consult."

"Cut the bull. You had better get over whatever problem you have with me and do what's right, and seeing that justice is done is what's right."

Standing up, Nancy looked Monica straight in the face and said, "Not if I have to work with the likes of you it's not." Brushing past Monica, she headed out of the courtroom.

Monica stifled the word "bitch" she felt straining to escape her mouth. Instead, she watched her leave the room. Rufus' mother was staring at her, confusion evident in her eyes. This whole situation was bizarre.

Perhaps she should speak to Judge DeLeone, but what would she look like saying, "The ADA is my cousin and she's passing for white and won't talk to me?" Screw that witch; she would get the last laugh when she won the case.

Nancy stepped out into the corridor and was side-swiped by a hand-holding young white couple rushing past. "Thanks a lot," she called after them. They entered the next courtroom down the hall without once looking back. "Idiots!"

Crossing over to the wall opposite the courtroom, she leaned against it, half expecting Monica to follow her out.

Her heart skipped a beat every time the door opened. If only she had gone to California when she had left home instead of New York. Glancing at her watch, she saw that she had four minutes remaining to herself. Then the courtroom door opened and the face that made her pulse race was that of Calvin James.

"Miss Michaels, I gotta talk to you," he said.

"What are you doing here?" Nancy whispered, her eyes nervously darting from one face to the next to see if anyone was observing them.

"I wanna know if you want me to try again now that you had time to think about it."

"I told you no this morning."

"Yeah, but I saw you and that lawyer talking just now. You looked upset. Did she say somethin' about last night?"

"Shut up," she said, grabbing Calvin by the arm and pulling him down the hall and out into the stairwell. Quickly releasing his arm, she began pushing the door to make it close faster.

"You real nervous, ain't you?"

"I don't want you coming to this court building again unless it's your case you're here for."

"Are you still gonna take care of my case?"

"This is not the place to talk about this and I told you I was. I'll get in touch with you this evening," she whispered, looking up and down the stairwell to see if anyone was there to overhear them.

"You backin out, ain't you?"

"I am not. I will keep my promise. Now, please leave."

"What about the money you promised?"

"That money was promised if you did the job. You didn't, so there's no money."

"Yeah, but I almost had her. I coulda got shot by that man that came runnin outta the buildin. I think I should at least get a thou for riskin my life."

"You must be joking."

"No, I'm not," he said, not smiling. "Do you wanna see my legs? They're swollen from that woman kickin me with the heels of her shoes. See, now that I know that she's a fighter, I know how to handle her next time."

"There will be no next time!" Nancy shrieked.

"All right. Damn. Calm down, will ya. Anyhow, I could use the money, I'm kinda broke."

The two stood facing each other less than two feet apart, their eyes locked, the meaning of his words unquestionably clear.

A tightness gripped Nancy's chest; the air in the stairwell was suddenly hot and thick like a sauna; her chest heaved. Undulating flashes of heat swept across her face and her neck. Unable to tear her eyes away from Calvin's face, Nancy reached up and wiped away the sweat that beaded up on her forehead.

"I have to get back into the courtroom right now. Can I call you on this later?"

"Sure can," Calvin James said smugly. "I'll be waitin to hear from you."

Chapter 17

"Without going into lengthy detail, Miss Michaels put the guy I suspect on the stand, but I reserved my right to interrogate him later, after I hear from Mr. Evans. Then the emotional cripple put the...."

"The emotional cripple?" Dayton asked.

"A.k.a Miss Nancy Michaels," Monica clarified for him before continuing. "She put the medical examiner on the stand and he testified that Madison's strangulation was brutally savage in that the killer snapped her neck for good measure."

"In other words, somebody made sure she was dead."

"In other words, overkill. When jurors hear such grisly details they look at the defendant through jaundiced eyes. I'm convinced of that."

"They're only human; I would too."

"Yes, but what if the person's not guilty?"

"That's what you're there for."

"I know. Additionally, when the examiner said that,

although Madison was not raped, her right nipple had been practically bitten off, every eye in the courtroom was on Rufus."

"Who else are they going to look at?"

"Just him. Which means, if Mr. Evans can't place Brown in Madison's block that morning, Rufus doesn't have a chance."

"Think positive. Who else testified today?"

"A criminal psychologist, who testified that the killer was likely to be a man who suffered from sexual dysfunction and was expert at cloaking his intense dislike for women. Miss Michaels tried to insinuate, based on the fight Rufus had with Brown, that Rufus was the killer. The psychologist also stated that the killer was capable of extreme anger, which goes without saying, and which is also true for ninety-five percent of mankind."

"He didn't paint too pretty a picture of the killer, did he?"

"Not at all. At least I hope it's not a picture of Rufus. It doesn't help that he keeps getting angry in court. His relationship with Madison was not platonic, which meant that he did not have to force himself on her. True, he was angry with her, but was he angry enough to bite off her nipple and strangle her to death? I don't think so."

"It appears that the psychologist's testimony might've scored points for the other side," Dayton suggested.

"Maybe. When the nipple was mentioned, Rufus closed his eyes. It looked to me like he was fighting back tears. The jury might've read it differently."

"I hope Mr. Evans comes through for you. By the way, what was it like between you and your cousin today?"

"Do you think I called her an emotional cripple for nothing? She reminds me of a person on the edge. The few times I've been face to face with her, she's been combative and nasty. I tried to talk to that witch about Brown and she stopped me cold. She said we had nothing to discuss and left me standing with egg on my face."

"She's a cold one, isn't she?"

"Like a glacier."

"It doesn't sound like she'll ever mellow."

"Please. The only time she'll mellow regarding me and my family will be when she's six feet under, and even then she'll probably wake up and check the coffins in the surrounding graves to see if they contain white bodies. Dayton, believe me, the woman's brain and soul are from another dimension. What's more, she might calm down if she'd only realize that I don't want to be related to anyone who hates me as deeply as she does. After this trial, I hope I never see her again. I pity her because, until the day she dies, she'll have a sadness that will eat away at her soul and she doesn't even know it."

"What does that mean?"

"It means that she gave up something that a majority of us experience only once in our lives. If we're lucky, maybe twice."

"What's that?"

"Unconditional love. Unconditional love from one's parents and, with God's blessing, unconditional love from our children are the greatest gifts a person can ever receive. I don't know if she has any children, but I know she turned her back on her parents."

"Do you know if they were ever abusive to her?"

"Dayton, if they were, I never saw it, which doesn't mean that it didn't happen. In this case, I doubt it. When

I did see them all together, Uncle Douglas and Aunt Wendy seemed to yearn for her to talk to them. They worshipped that girl. They probably would've settled for a pat on the head if she would've had the heart and sensitivity to give them one."

"You know what I don't understand? If her behavior was so blatantly disrespectful, why didn't someone talk to her and at least attempt to straighten her out?"

"Are you kidding? No one dared say anything to upset DeeAnn. Oh, my mother wanted to slap her upside the head a few times, but my uncle wouldn't hear of it."

"Did you say she had a brother? How did he get along with her?"

"Winston? They had no relationship. He should be about twenty-five now. I hear he got a masters in accounting last year. He used to come over to the house a lot to hang out with Kevin. My mother says that the two of them are quite close these days. I think it's sweet."

"Did Winston ever talk about DeeAnn to you?"

"Nope. Maybe he talked to Kevin, but really, what was there to talk about? She was a big bore, stuck on herself, which she apparently hasn't outgrown."

"You seem so angry."

"I am. Talking about her makes me angry. On one hand I pity her, but I dislike her even more."

"Look at you; you're stressing yourself out."

"And I'm beginning to get a headache. Look, I don't want to talk about that woman anymore. From what little I can see, she's living the life she wants. I just hope she's happy."

Getting up from his chair, Dayton stepped around Monica's desk and slid behind her chair, his back touching the wall. "Your face looks so tense. Rest your head on the back of the chair; I'll give you a massage."

She sighed when Dayton began gently massaging the tension from her forehead. Her arms hanging at her sides, she closed her eyes and dissolved under his touch.

"I could hear you moaning all the way down the hall. It sounds like something illicit is going on in here," Mr. Evans said, coming into Monica's office. "It's a good thing everyone's gone for the day."

Monica slowly opened her eyes.

Continuing to lightly run his fingers over Monica's forehead, Dayton asked, "How you doing, man?"

"Good! I'm doing real good. It's been a long time. How's life by you?" Mr. Evans asked, extending his right hand.

"Good," Dayton said, shaking his hand, then returning to massaging Monica's temple and forehead.

"You two look real cozy together. An old-timer told me once that a man doesn't get married until a woman lets him know it's time. Are those wedding bells ready to sound yet, or hasn't she asked you yet?"

Sensing a slight hesitation in Dayton's massaging, Monica raised her head and gave Mr. Evans a piercing glare. He smiled innocently.

Dayton came from behind Monica's chair and sat down again in the chair across from her desk.

Monica quickly relaxed her glare and smiled instead. "You have something, don't you? You're grinning like a Cheshire cat."

"Sure do," he said, sauntering over to the desk near the window and hoisting his ample body atop it and settling himself. "I'm glad Dayton came to wait with you."

"Will you please tell me what you have before I burst wide open."

"Do you find her impatient?"

"I'm not in this," Dayton said, crossing his right leg over his left thigh.

"You should marry this guy. He already knows not to speak against you."

Sucking her teeth, Monica said to Dayton, "You know he only does this to me. With every other attorney around here, he's to the point. With me, he makes me wait with bated breath for his information. I think he likes to see me frustrated, which I think is cruel. One of these days, I'm gonna clock him. Mr. Evans, please."

"The car was on the block," he said, smiling broadly.

"*Yes*! A big one for the home team," Monica cheered, slapping the palms of her hands on her desk repeatedly.

"Congratulations to the both of you," Dayton said.

"Thank you," Mr. Evan responded, bowing his head slightly.

"So humble, so modest. You deserve a Congressional Medal of Honor for this one. How did you do it?" Monica asked.

"They don't call a policeman 'flatfoot' for nothing. I beat the hell outta those sidewalks on Hancock Street from Sumner down to Nostrand Avenue. I even went a block on either side of Hancock on every avenue down to Nostrand—just in case Brown turned the corner instead of going straight. The city might have to repave the whole damn stretch."

"You're funny," Monica laughed.

"I wasn't funny when I was pounding those damn sidewalks. I checked stores that weren't even open that night in case someone heard about something."

"Who saw the car?" Monica asked excitedly.

Ignoring Monica's question, Mr. Evans continued his

story. "I went back this afternoon and early this evening in case I missed someone during the morning hours. My feet are killing me."

"Dayton has great hands; he'll massage your feet later."

"What?" Dayton quickly asked.

"Relax, just joking. Mr. Evans, I'll buy you a foot soak and massager for Christmas if you tell me immediately who saw the car."

"Two people."

"You're kidding."

"That's right. An old lady named Myrtle Henderson, a chronic insomniac for the past twenty-five years who lives at the corner of Hancock and Sumner over a store, and—you're gonna faint when you hear this one— Brendalynn Lenox."

"Did I hear you right?"

"Yep. The same woman you interrogated yesterday. She said a lot of unkind, ugly things about you, lady."

"Like who cares? I wasn't interviewing her for a job as my friend. What did she see?"

"Firstly, it took me awhile to get her to open up. When she thought I was working for you, she didn't wanna talk. So I told her that she misunderstood and that I was working for the court."

"Oh great. So what happens when she's called as a witness for the defense?"

"Have her declared a hostile witness and eat her up alive. As I was saying, I told her that I wanted to know if she heard a car making any excessive noise pulling out of the block the night of the murder. See, I learned that the muffler on the Seville was and still is loud. There's a big hole in the muffler. It didn't take her long

165

to remember that a red car with a black top, sounding like a motorcycle, started up approximately twenty minutes after Washington left the building. The car started but apparently shut off when the driver tried to pull off. Get this, he was parked right in front of the building."

"But a lot of cars are loud. I hear them all the time myself, but I don't run to my window. What made her get up and look out the window?" Monica asked.

"The noise. She was watching television and the window was open. It was still pretty warm out."

"That's right. *Showtime at the Apollo* was on."

"Right. The noise was drowning out the show. She said that the driver gunned the engine to keep the car running. That's when she looked out the window. She saw the car for about a minute before it peeled away from the front of the house—with no headlights."

"Did she see the driver?"

"We're not that lucky. She was looking down on the car, but she said the car was red and black."

"If the car was so loud, why didn't she hear it when it pulled up in the first place?"

"Because, she said, it didn't seem as loud for some reason. It's possible that the driver pulled up as Washington was slamming the door downstairs and Lenox was in the hallway herself yelling at him."

"This is too good to be true. I'm so glad I put off questioning Brown." Monica said, jumping up from her chair. "What about the other woman?"

"Hold on. Lenox also said that, just after the car sped away, she heard a crash at the corner of Hancock and Sumner."

"That explains the damage on the car."

"It gets even better. This is where Mrs. Henderson

comes in. Her bed is next to the window overlooking that very same intersection. Since she rarely sleeps, she placed her bed so she could see the street and still watch television. In fact, the bed is right under the window."

"Great candidate for a block watch," Dayton said flippantly.

"No joke. She reports everything illegal she sees to the police. On the twenty-fourth, after one in the morning, she heard a car roaring down Hancock toward Sumner. By the way, there are no traffic lights at that corner. The red and black car, with no lights, ran the stop sign and was struck on the passenger side rear by a small white car coming down Sumner. By the way, Sumner Avenue is a one way street, just as Hancock is. The red car with the black top, as she and Lenox both describe it, stopped momentarily, straightened out and took off, going straight down Hancock towards Troop Avenue. The driver of the white car was madder than 'worms during a flood.' Mrs. Henderson's words. The front end of his car was totaled."

"Did he give chase?"

"No. Seems he got out of his car, but by the time he realized that the other driver wasn't going to do likewise, the red car had roared off. His car had to be towed."

"If the driver filed an accident report, then we're home free."

"He did, at the seven nine."

"You're on the case."

"Yes, I am. I used my contacts to get the report. Not an easy task to do after all this time. The driver was a Willis Sloan and, like a lot of men, he knows his cars. The report didn't show a license number for the car, but Sloan identified the car as a red four-door 1976 Cadillac Seville with a black vinyl roof. Can't get no better than that."

"What was Sloan driving?"

"A 1988 Pontiac Grand Am."

"We have to bring him in as a witness. This is unbelievable!" Monica said, coming from behind her desk and going over to stand next to Mr. Evans.

"Can't."

"Can't what?"

"Mr. Sloan died back in January."

"Oh my. Was his death a result of the accident?"

"Nope. I got his address off the report. I went to his apartment and his son said he died of a heart attack. He had a history of heart problems."

"His testimony would have slammed the door on this case."

"It still can. I have a copy of the accident report right here," Mr. Evans said, taking the report from inside his jacket pocket and handing it to Monica. "And get this, Sloan's son says that, after the Seville sped off, his father found a splash guard that came off the car. Sloan kept it in the trunk of his car hoping to one day run across the Seville again. And yes, Baptiste's car is missing a splash guard on the passenger side rear."

"Does his son have the car?"

"The car was turned over to the bank after his death."

"Shoot."

"Was there anything special about the splash guard?" Dayton asked.

"The ones on the car are red with the silhouette of a naked woman sitting pretty."

"Are they common?" Dayton asked.

"I don't see them much, but they're out there. Monica, you can thank your lucky stars. His son took everything out of the trunk of the car and put it in a box in his aunt's basement. I asked him to check the box for the splash guard. He's more than happy to do it. Some kind of satisfaction for getting the man back that caused that accident. He'll beep me if he finds it. The other three are still on the car; we can get them.

"Let's keep our fingers crossed. Without that guard the rest don't mean a thing," Monica said, returning to her desk and jotting quickly. "Can either one of the women identify the Seville if they saw it again? It has been eight months you know."

"I think so. Earlier this morning, I drove to Baptiste's house before going onto Hancock and took some instants of the car. I was afraid at first that they wouldn't be able to identify it, but they did. If need be, we can seize the car. By the way, as I told you yesterday, it's still banged up on that side. Baptiste didn't have the money to repair it or the muffler. The car is just something for him to get around in."

"You're good," Dayton said.

"Just doing my job."

"A job that will win this case for me."

"Take some credit yourself. You went with your client's accusation about Brown and put me on to tracking him."

"Yes, but you knew enough to track down his friends, and…."

"And I'll gladly take the credit for both of you," Dayton offered. "You're both great. Now, where do you go from here?"

Continuing to write as she spoke, Monica said, "I need to first get subpoenas for both women, which are to be served first thing tomorrow morning."

"No problem."

"Good. Baptiste was served this morning. Tonight I have to prepare my questions for the two women and Baptiste and Brown. May I review your notes?"

"Sure, I knew you'd want them, so I took the time to rewrite them more clearly," he said, passing the folded papers to Dayton, who handed them to Monica.

Taking the notes, Monica continued writing. "Also, I have to notify the Department of Corrections that I want Brown back in court tomorrow. Placing Brown at the scene will establish reasonable doubt in the minds of the jurors. Oh, and I mustn't forget, notify the DA's office of unscheduled witnesses and new evidence. No time for mistakes. We don't want a mistrial. Do you fellas realize that my entire defense strategy has changed. I love it. I can't wait 'til tomorrow."

Chapter 18

Forestalling the inevitable—going home—by staying in the office long after the trash cans were emptied did nothing to abate the overwhelming anxiety that had filled Nancy since her meeting with Calvin James. With Robert away, there was nothing to rush home to anyway. Though he was rarely home before her, she always knew that he would be coming home. This was the third time in two years that they had been apart, yet this separation dredged up the awful loneliness of the days and years she spent in self-imposed isolation in her bedroom.

Going home also meant having to call Calvin James. She had called his house once around seven fifteen and was relieved when no one answered the phone. She almost didn't make that call, but fear that he might show up in court again prompted her to get his number from its hiding place under the leather flap in her wallet.

The way her luck had been going, it was no surprise that she walked into the apartment at the tail end of

Robert's call from Dallas. The volume on the answering machine was turned up and Robert was saying, "I'll call you again later." She had raced to pick up the phone, but a dial tone was the only response to her calling, "Robert, Robert," before the machine beeped. She rewound the tape and listened to his message.

"Hi, Nancy. If you're there, pick up. You're not? Okay. We arrived in Dallas around eleven o'clock this morning and went straight to Alcoa headquarters. We've been meeting ever since. It's too early to gauge the outcome of the merger. However, it does look good for our client. At the rate we're moving along, contractual snags might be worked out in a few days. I hope your trial is going well. Have to get back now. I'll call you again later," he said, his voice sounding annoyingly humdrum.

"That's it? No phone number? No hotel?" Nancy asked angrily, throwing her pocketbook and briefcase on the couch. Shaking her head and sighing, she stood staring at the telephone. Tears were beginning to well up in her eyes.

Being a loner had always suited her, until now. She had always resolved her problems without benefit of discussion or input from another human being, but now she wished someone could tell her how to get out of the tangled web that she herself had woven. What was she to do about Calvin James? Suppose his demands didn't stop after she paid him? If she didn't meet his demands, would he tell Monica or the police about her plot to be rid of her?

"Why is my life so screwed up?" Nancy cried mournfully, pressing her hands to her mouth to muffle the gut-wrenching sobs that leaped from her throat. Running to the bathroom and slamming the door behind her, she turned on both the hot and cold water faucets full force in the bathtub. She didn't know if she could be heard by anyone, but she hoped that the rushing sound of water would drown out her cries. Sitting down on the toilet seat, hugging her body, rocking back and forth, she cried deep from within her being. She cried until her head pounded from the strain. It was the pain in her head that stopped her crying, but the crying had relieved the tightness in her chest and stomach. A welcome calm settled over her body. From the medicine cabinet she took out a bottle of aspirin. Popping two in her mouth, she drank water from her hand cupped under the sink faucet.

Turning off the water in the tub, Nancy stood at the sink, splashing her face with cold water. Thinking that she heard the telephone ring, she quickly shut off the water and listened keenly for the ringing. There was none. Drying her face with her towel, she studied herself in the mirror. Her eyes were pink and puffy, her nose red. Her hair hung wet and limp around her face. The strain was taking its toll; she looked older. Taking her towel out of the bathroom with her, she blotted at her hair as she went into the bedroom and sat on Robert's side of the bed near his nightstand, where the telephone sat. Kicking off her pumps, she lay down and curled up on the bed.

Looking over at the telephone Nancy said softly, "Robert, please call."

"*Buzzzzzzz!*" It was the doorbell.

Sitting bolt upright, she threw her legs over the side of the bed. She wasn't expecting anyone, and it was the exception if anyone happened by.

"*Buzzzzzzz!*"

In her stocking feet, she raced to the apartment door

and opened it. She refrained from pressing the buzzer to open the downstairs door. There were four apartments in the brownstone and everyone's name was under their bells. Whoever it was ought to read the names.

"*Buzzzzzzz!*"

Stepping out into the hallway, Nancy turned and pushed the button on the door's edge—disabling the slam lock—before she ran nimbly down the one flight of carpeted stairs to the main floor. She tried peeking from behind the white lace curtains at the inside door, but the outer door also had white lace curtains which, because of the darkness outside, she couldn't see through.

"*Buzzzzzzz!*" sounded faintly overhead.

Cautiously opening the door, she stepped out onto the cold mosaic tile. Pulling back the lace curtain on the outer door unveiled the boyish, grinning face of Calvin James. Inhaling sharply, Nancy yanked the curtain closed. Her heart quivered.

Calvin James rapped on the glass.

A tingling sensation crept along Nancy's arms; goose bumps sprouted. Rubbing both arms simultaneously, she tried to rub away the tingling. How in the world did he find out where she lived?

The rapping came again.

Nancy snatched the curtain back and glared bullets at Calvin James.

"Hey, whut's up?" he said, grinning.

"What the hell do you mean what's up?"

"You know, whut's up? See, I needs the money t'night. I ain't inconveniencing you, am I?"

"How dare you come here! How did you know where I lived?"

"Whut you say? I can't hear you through the door," Calvin James said, pointing to his ears and shaking his head.

Nancy stared at him. Her intense hate for him labored her breathing.

"I hope you ain't tryin to kill me wit'cha evil looks. I ain't plannin' to stay for dinner. I just wants ma money, then I'm outta here."

"I said I would contact you. How did you get my address?"

"I didn't believe you'd call. I followed you from downtown. The jolly green giant could've followed you, you walk the streets like you lost in space."

Nancy stared at the threat before her; this was a face that she would remember the rest of her life.

"Plus," he continued, "I called home and my mother didn't say you called, so I decided to do a eyeball to eyeball."

"I did call. Neither you nor your mother were home. I was about to try you again. Please leave, I'll call you in an hour."

"You can save the quarter. I'm here now. Give me the green and I'll show you my back."

"This is crazy. I don't have the money on me."

"You can get it."

"Wait a damn minute. I will not be pressured…."

"Naw, man, you can't help me," Calvin James said to someone coming up the stairs behind him.

Nancy looked to the left of Calvin James and saw her neighbor, Steve Kramer, who shared the apartment on the top floor with an older man. The more effeminate of the two, Steve was a chatterbox who often cornered her to talk about plants or a new recipe he'd discovered.

Nancy quickly unlocked the door.

"Are you looking for someone? Perhaps I can help you," Steve offered.

Calvin James gave Steve the once over and side-stepped away from him. "Naw, man, there ain't a thing you can do to help me."

"Steve. Hello. It's all right. He's a messenger from my office. You know, special trial. It's a worknight for me," Nancy lied.

"Pardon me, brother; one can't be too careful. You understand," Steve said awkwardly, extending his hand.

Calvin James, giving Steve a fake toothy grin, stuffed his hands in his jacket pockets, saying, "I ain't yo brother."

Steve drew back his hand and glanced questioningly at Nancy. "Nancy, I'll get out of your way. You must come up to see us sometime."

"I will. Have a good evening," she said, swallowing to wet her throat.

"Night night," Calvin James said in a soft, high pitched voice.

Steve ignored the slur and bounded up the stairs out of sight.

"Look, I gotta...."

"Shhhhhh! Please," Nancy demanded, her head inclined toward the stairs, listening for Steve's footfalls. When the door above slammed shut, she pulled the inside door up behind her and, careful to not lock herself out, stepped outside onto the stoop. The stone was colder and rougher underfoot than the tile. An icy chill shot up the back of her legs.

"Give me the money. I gots to go."

"You get nothing if you don't lower your voice and

keep it that way. In fact, come away from the door," she said, running down the cold stone stairs to the sidewalk. Calvin James followed. "I told you, I don't have that amount of money on hand."

"Yeah, but you can get it."

"No, I can't. Not at this hour. The banks are closed."

"I ain't stupid. I know that. And I also know that you got one of those bank machine cards."

"But...."

"There ain't no buts. Just get the plastic and get my money."

"I don't think I have enough in my checking account to draw on," Nancy said, realizing that there was no way out.

"You white; you got a savings account."

In a sick way, she wanted to thank him for acknowledging her as white, but on the other hand she was ticked off by his assumption. "I have you know that being white is not synonymous with having money. A lot of us are just as poor as you blacks."

"Well us blacks in the ghetto don't know that. You white people got it that way. Take the money from your savings account; I know you got one."

"You presume a lot. You don't know what my resources are. What's more, I don't know why I'm standing here haggling with the likes of you about what I do and don't have. If I give you a cent, it's for your time and trouble. And I strongly suggest that you don't get any further ideas about getting anything else out of me or waste your time or mine with some stupid threats. Take my word for it, you won't walk away unscathed. In addition to attempted abduction, there will be charges of blackmail. Never mind the fact that you are currently up on charges of first-degree burglary," she said, rallying in courage as she always did when she was backed up against the wall. It would have helped if she could've seen his face clearer to know if her threats were registering, but they were standing in the shadow of a large fully clothed tree, which blocked the rays of the streetlight.

"So whatever you have in mind for me, forget it. There will be no further contact with me once you get your money. Is that clear?"

Unmoved, Calvin James, looming over her as it was, sidled up closer to Nancy, forcing her to step back. "I told you befo', I ain't stupid. You white people think y'all got all the brains. I understands the words, but check out my words. There's people who'd jump on the 411 that you tried to use me to get rid of your competition—a sister. And from what I can see, a sister that might whip your ass."

Nancy flinched when he pointed his finger in her face.

"I might get in deep and might even do some time, but I can deal with life behind bars. Can you? Do you think your white ass can do the time? You definitely did the crime."

A chilling, prickly sensation eased up Nancy's back into the nape of her neck. A sour, bitter taste rose from her empty stomach into her throat and sickened her. The question needed no answer. Death was more inviting than a jail cell, but for the Calvin Jameses of the world, life behind bars was a vacation from working the streets. The fearless seventeen-year-old boy manipulating her life completely unnerved her. He could do more damage to her life than she could to his. She had to give him something to appease him, but a thousand dollars wasn't what she had in mind.

"If I go to the bank with my ATM card, I can only withdraw five hundred dollars in any one day," she lied, knowing that a thousand dollars was the maximum.

"No sweat. I'll take the five now and you can get the other five in the morning befo you go to work. I can meet you at the bank or downtown; I goes with the flow."

"Don't do me any favors. If it means breaking into the bank, I'll have all of your money tonight. I don't want to ever see you again after this night."

"And I thought you liked me. You'll have to see me in court when ma case come up next month."

Going back towards the stairs, Nancy responded, "Believe me, I won't even see you then."

"That's all right, as long as you fix my case," he said, rubbing his hands together. "Right now, let's get busy."

"Do you mind if I get my shoes and my card?"

"No, baby, I don't mind. You gets what you needs, I'm chillin' right here 'til you come back," he said, sitting down at the bottom of the stairs and looking up at her.

"And I will go into the bank alone. You'll wait a block away."

"Naw, you might pull a fast one."

"A fast one like what? You know where I live. That's my condition. Take it or leave it."

"You tough. Can't nobody say you ain't tough. No problem. I'm a lamp post, lean on me."

Disgusted, Nancy peered down at him.

"You look like you smell something stank."

"I do," she said, running swiftly up the flight of stairs into the building and locking the doors behind her.

Still in her work clothes, Nancy lay on the living room sofa curled up in a tight ball after returning home from the bank. The sobbing had long since stopped, yet tears still emptied from her eyes. When she gave Calvin James the money, she threw the wad of bills at his chest and ran. She never looked back to see if he had to scrounge around on the ground in the dark for the money, but she heard him shout, "Bitch! It's like that huh? Bet!" She never looked back to see if he was coming after her.

Once back in the apartment, she had stood watch at the living room window biting her thumb knuckle to keep from screaming. If she could have one wish, it would be that Calvin James would drop dead along with Monica. After ten minutes he had not come up the street from Seventh Avenue. That was when she breathed a sigh of relief, when her heart stopped pounding. Her strength deserted her and she fell onto the living room sofa.

The surreal glow from the night light in the hallway gave off just enough light for her to make out the time on the wall clock. It was well past ten o'clock and Robert still had not called. In her haste to be rid of Calvin James, she had left the apartment without turning the answering machine back on. Even if she missed Robert's call, he had to know that she would be home waiting to hear from him. It wasn't like she had anywhere to go. She understood that he was busy, but being busy did not justify his not calling again or his not leaving a telephone number where she could reach him. If he didn't call again, she would call his office in the morning and get the hotel and the number where he was staying in Dallas.

Willingly, she slipped into the sweet, sometimes protective arms of sleep.

Chapter 19

"What have we covered for the past forty minutes that you and I both agree on, Mr. Brown? That you, until September 24, 1989, owned a red, four-door 1976 Cadillac Seville with a black vinyl roof and a noisy muffler. We also agree that, after the party where you had a fight with defendant over decedent, your ex-girl friend, you went to a social club, minutes away from Charlene Madison's apartment, with three of your friends. Whom I might add, you left behind before one A.M. to go home, despite the fact that they live on the same block as you and despite the fact that you were on good terms with all three."

"I can go home by myself," Brown snapped.

"Home is a convenient place to go, especially when one lives alone and there is no one to confirm or deny one's presence there."

"Can you say I didn't? You wusn't there."

"Neither were you."

"Says who?"

"Objection. Where is this line of questioning leading?" Nancy asked. At this point she didn't care what Monica did in court as long as the process moved along and this trial ended. This line of questioning, however, was annoying and dragging.

"Counselor, where are you going with this?" Judge DeLeone asked.

"Your honor, if the court will bear with me, I will show that witness knows more about what happened to decedent that fateful evening than he has admitted."

"Continue. However, I hope relevance will soon be clear."

Shaking her head, Nancy recrossed her legs.

"It will, your honor."

Brown yawned openly in Monica's face.

Monica briefly covering her nose and mouth with her right hand, then continued. "What we don't agree on is, between the time you left the social club and the time you sold the car to Daniel Baptiste on that same Sunday morning, how the car came to be damaged. Mr. Baptiste says the car was damaged when he bought it. You say it wasn't. There is testimony that you went to Charlene Madison's apartment to get reacquainted. You say you didn't. I believe you were in a car accident that Sunday morning. You say you don't remember. I believe you left town unexpectedly; you say you planned it."

"You got it."

"Let's see if I do, Mr. Brown. Earlier the court heard testimony that on Sunday, September 24, 1989, your car was parked in front of 531B Hancock Street at one-twenty A.M."

"Says who? That ain't the only '76 Seville in the

world. That coulda been anybody's car. Did somebody see me? Can't nobody say they seen me."

The gavel was banged once. Brown looked up at Judge DeLeone and then smugly back at Monica.

"There is also testimony that the car was unusually loud, especially at that time of night. The car was driven off with the lights off at one-twenty A.M. and collided with a white car at the corner of Hancock Street and Sumner Avenue, down the street from Charlene Madison's apartment."

"And that wus supposed to be me, right?"

"You tell me. It seems the driver of the Seville ran the stop sign. Were you the driver of that Seville, Mr. Brown?" Monica asked, taking a sheet of paper from between the pages of her legal pad.

"Nope. My name is Wes, I wasn't in that mess."

Ignoring Brown, Monica approached the bench. "Your honor, I admit into evidence defense exhibit D, an accident report dated September 24, 1989."

Briefly reviewing the report, Judge DeLeone stated, "Marked and entered."

Monica turned to present the report to the prosecutor, but Nancy looked down at her notes. Shrugging her shoulders, Monica dropped the report on the table and turned again to face Brown.

"What I have here is an accident report filed by a Mr. Willis Sloan on the Sunday morning in question. The time of the accident is listed as one-twenty-five A.M. The two vehicles involved in the collision were a 1976 Cadillac Seville and a 1988 Pontiac Grand Am. The color of the Seville is listed as red with a black vinyl roof. The accident is listed as a hit and run. Again, Mr. Brown, were you the driver of that car?"

"Again, *no*!"

"This is your last warning, Mr. Brown; raise your voice again, and you will be held in contempt of court."

Brown smirked, slouching lower in his chair.

"Here, in defense exhibits A and C, the Seville has three identical splash guards behind each wheel except the passenger side rear," Monica explained, showing the pictures to Judge DeLeone and to Delroy Brown. Going over to the defense table, she picked up a plastic shopping bag from under the table.

"Your honor, I admit into evidence defense exhibits E, F, and G. These splash guards are the ones shown in the photographs and were taken off the Seville just this morning. Each splash guard is tagged indicating which position it came from."

Brown began chuckling low at first; then, throwing his head back, he laughed heartily.

Judge DeLeone tapped the gavel repeatedly. "Mr. Brown, you're in contempt of this court. You will pay. Get control of yourself."

Brown covered his mouth with his hand and snickered. Judge DeLeone narrowed his gaze at him.

"Also, your honor," Monica continued, turning away from the witness stand, "I'm admitting into evidence defense exhibit H, the splash guard retrieved from the scene of the accident by the late Willis Sloan, who was driving the 1988 Pontiac Grand Am. Your honor, it is an exact match."

"Objection. The people were not informed of the evidence presented in this court, and there is no proof that these guards in fact came off the car in question. I therefore move to suppress."

"Your honor, evidence was not located until two hours

ago. A warrant was duly executed and the splash guards were removed in the presence of two officers from the New York City Police Department. They are prepared to testify. Their sworn depositions are forthcoming. Defense did not purposely withhold evidence."

"Motion denied; evidence entered as defense exhibits E, F, G, and H."

"Exception," Nancy stated.

"Noted," Judge DeLeone responded.

"Thank you, your honor," Monica said, turning to Brown again. "Mr. Brown, why don't we stop wasting the court's time. These splash guards came off the Seville you once owned. Mr. Baptiste did not buy them, he did not replace them. In fact, he drives the car today just as you sold it to him eight months ago. I submit that you, Mr. Brown, were involved in that accident that Sunday morning, running the stop sign because you were in a hurry. I equally submit that you were in the Madison apartment prior to the accident. I contend that you entered the apartment building through the unlocked front doors, unobserved, after defendant left at one A.M. And I believe you may have even seen defendant leave."

"Objection. Pure speculation," Nancy announced. "Counsel is conjecturing."

Brown, laughing silently, mugged at Monica and flipped his hand at her.

"Mr. Brown," Judge DeLeone said, pointing his finger at him as a warning.

Brown sat up at attention immediately, while pressing his lips together to suppress his laughter.

"Objection noted, but I would like counsel to continue."

Nodding to the judge, Monica turned to the witness stand.

"Miss Madison opened the apartment door to you, Mr. Brown, because you were an old friend, didn't she? She was angry with her boyfriend and you were, supposedly, a friendly face."

Brown continued pressing his lips together, his body jerking as if he were having a good laugh.

"Did you kill Charlene Madison?"

"You know everything; you tell me," he jeered

"Once inside the apartment, Mr. Brown, did Miss Madison have apprehensions about your intentions? You were not there to console a friend, were you? When you realized that she was home alone, you tried to seduce her into having sex with you, didn't you? She rejected you, didn't she?"

"Objection. Gross speculation and unsupported evidence. Your honor, how much longer must the court be subjected to this line of frivolous questioning?" Nancy asked.

"Your honor, as the prosecutor is well aware, in the best interest of my client, I have the right to establish reasonable doubt. The possibility that this witness could have committed this crime is not unlikely. Hence, questions proving that possibility are not frivolous."

"Establishing reasonable doubt on the back of this witness when there is no evidence of his having committed the crime is a waste of time."

"Proving evidence of witness' physical presence in the immediate vicinity of a crime is not, by my estimation, considered a waste of time."

Judge DeLeone tapped his gavel. "That's enough. Overruled. Miss Hall, move on."

Nancy dropped her pen onto the table.

Brown stopped snickering.

186

Voices rose throughout the room. Banging the gavel twice, Judge DeLeone called for order. It was quiet immediately.

"Charlene didn't want you making love to her did she? You were hot for her, but she was cold; maybe even repulsed by you. She wasn't turned on by the dance or by seeing you again, was she?"

"Objection. Badgering the witness."

"Sustained. You're out of bounds, counselor."

"I'm sorry, your honor," Monica said, stepping back from the witness stand.

Brown, his mouth moving soundlessly, shifted repeatedly in his chair.

Sighing deeply, Monica reviewed her notes. "Mr. Brown...."

"Careful, counselor," Judge DeLeone warned.

Nodding in acknowledgment of the warning, Monica stepped back up to the witness stand, purposely standing directly in front of Brown.

"Decedent was bitten savagely on the right nipple, apparently after death. Forensic science is quite interesting, Mr. Brown. Did you know that a mold was made of the teeth marks on decedent's nipple and breast?"

Brown's eyes widened.

"Did you know that dried saliva from the nipple and breast was gathered and preserved?"

Brown glared at Monica.

"Did you know that those teeth marks and the analyzed saliva can be matched with the killer? All the court has to do is order samples of saliva and bite marks from suspects. Imagine, it works just like fingerprinting. My client has willingly given samples. The court can order that you do likewise."

"The hell I won't."

"Why not?"

"I got rights...."

"Yes, but so did Charlene Madison. Whoever killed her took away her right to live. When she turned you down, were you so angry that you killed her? Did you kill her because she didn't have fond memories of love-making with you? Apparently you're not as good in bed as you thought you were. Perhaps quite forgettable, if anything."

"Counselor!"

"Objection!"

"You bitch!" Brown shouted, bolting out of his chair and lunging at Monica, forcing her to jump back out of his reach. "If I get my hands around your goddamn throat, I'll choke the hell out of you too!"

Prison guards and court officers charged Brown and wrestled him to the floor inside the witness box.

"I told you he did it!" Rufus shouted, jumping up out of his chair. "I told you!"

Monica rushed over to the defense table and pushed Rufus back down into his seat. "Sit down. It's not over yet."

Rufus sat but said excitedly, "I knew he did it. I knew it!"

The gavel echoed throughout the room over the rumblings from the spectators, some of whom were now standing.

"Order in this courtroom! Mr. Brown, I order you to keep your mouth shut until you have been read your rights and have had the benefit of counsel!"

Nancy quickly packed up her briefcase. There would be no point in her questioning the witness.

Breathless, and though his face was pressed to the floor and his voice muffled and strained, Brown shouted, "You know what you can do with those damn rights! I killed the stupid bitch! Whutcho gonna do 'bout it? Lock me up? I'm already locked up! Big deal!"

"Get that man out of here!" Judge DeLeone bellowed at the officers while continually banging his gavel for silence. "Everyone sit down and be quiet!"

Monica waited until everyone had quieted down before she said, "Move to dismiss, your honor, based on evidence presented before the court and on witness' confession."

"Put it in writing, counselor, and get it to me before six this evening or I will not sign until Monday morning. Miss Hall, do not perform like that in my court again. Ladies and gentlemen of the jury, thank you for your service to this court. You're dismissed. Court's adjourned."

The crack of the gavel bounced off the walls.

No sooner had Judge DeLeone exited the courtroom than Rufus shouted, "All right!" He reached over and grabbed Monica, hugging her tightly. "Thank you, Miss Hall!"

"You're welcome," Monica said when he released her.

"Thank you, thank you, thank you," Mrs. Washington said behind Monica.

"Can I go home now?"

"Not yet. A motion to dismiss will have to be filed, which the judge will sign as soon as I can get it written and typed. If not today, can you wait until Monday morning? You'll be released immediately after that."

"That's all right. I can do these last few days in a minute, long as I know I'm getting out."

"Good. Go with the officers now and I'll see you real soon."

"Thank you, Miss Hall," Rufus said gleefully before he was led away.

Monica wasn't surprised to see that the prosecutor's chair was empty.

"You did good, kid," Mr. Evans said. "Great move with the teeth marks and the saliva. You went for the jugular like a high-powered legal shark."

"I did my best, but then you know I couldn't have done it without you."

"With or without me, that was a beauty to behold."

"Excuse me, Miss Hall. My name is Calvin James. I gotta talk to you for a minute."

"Do I know you?"

"No, but I got something for you."

Chapter 20

Nancy could see before she got halfway up the stairs that the door to the apartment was wide open. Startled, she stood on the stairs thinking that she had been burglarized, but then Robert suddenly appeared at the door just as she started back down the stairs.

"Robert."

"Hi."

Running quickly up the stairs, she dropped her briefcase to the floor and flung herself into his arms.

"I'm so glad to see you," she said, clutching and kissing him passionately. "Why didn't you call me back last night?"

"I didn't get another opportunity. I couldn't get away from the meeting. It was a marathon session; even our meals were served during the meeting," he said, holding her in his arms for an extended moment before kissing her gently on the lips and stepping out of her embrace.

"I missed you."

Bending and picking up Nancy's briefcase, Robert said nothing as he backed into the apartment and waited for Nancy to step inside before he closed the door. Setting the briefcase on the chair in the living room, he asked, "Everything all right?"

Her elation quickly faded. A chill seemed to embrace her heart.

"Is everything all right with you?"

"Yes, of course."

He seemed to be at a loss for something to say. His eyes wandered around the apartment. Stuffing his hands inside his pants pockets, he smiled weakly.

Her eyes never leaving Robert's face, Nancy laid her pocketbook on top of her briefcase and, removing her jacket, laid it across the back of the chair. Perhaps he was tired.

"Did you eat dinner?" he asked finally.

"No. I was thinking about making a tuna salad."

"Do you want to go out for dinner?"

"I'd rather stay in with you."

"What say I go out for Chinese or pizza?"

"Your choice."

"I'll get my jacket," he said, heading for the bedroom.

Taken aback by his aloofness, Nancy followed him into the bedroom.

"Are you all right?"

"Yes. Why?"

"You seem a little distant."

Again Robert was silent.

Perplexed, Nancy sat down on the bed. "Did something go wrong with the negotiations? You weren't due back for several days. What happened?"

"The negotiations went well. There is no doubt that the merger will happen. I came back early because there are contractual documents that must be prepared here from our offices. I'm returning Sunday night. How about you? How is the trial progressing?"

"Mercifully, it's all over."

"Jury out already?"

"It won't go to jury. A witness confessed."

"Really? I thought that only happened in the movies."

"I use to think that myself."

"Who confessed?"

"I don't want to talk about that right now. If all went well with you, why are you acting so strange?"

He started to respond but instead shook his head and ran his fingers through his hair.

"Robert?"

Leaving his jacket on the hook on the back of the door, he went and sat down next to Nancy on the bed.

"What's wrong?" she asked anxiously, trying to look into his eyes, but his head was bowed and his eyes downcast.

"Robert?"

Slowly he looked up into her eyes.

She could see a sadness in his eyes that she had only seen once before, when his grandmother had died.

"Nancy, I have to tell you something that I would give anything not to have to say."

"Has someone died?"

"No."

"Are you sick?"

"Nancy, listen to me. While I have the courage, please let me talk. I've waited as long as I could, hoping that what I was feeling was a mistake."

"A mistake? What does that mean?"

"I never wanted to hurt you. I had always seen my future through your eyes, but...."

Dumbfounded, Nancy gaped at him. Suddenly she sprang up off the bed. "No..., no! I don't want to hear this," she said, moving away from Robert and shaking both her head and her hands no.

"I'm so sorry. I didn't mean for this to happen," he said, leaning forward and resting his elbows on the top of his thighs, his hands clasped so tightly his knuckles turned white.

"You're sorry for what? What are you sorry for?"

Robert didn't answer. Instead, he shook his head.

"What are you sorry for?" she demanded. "

Without looking up, he said, "I'm in love with someone else."

"*What*?"

"Nancy, believe me; I didn't mean for this to happen."

Staggering backwards towards the window, gaping at Robert, Nancy felt behind her for the chair. Touching it, she slumped into it.

"I know this comes as a shock to you, but I fought with all my might not to have this happen. I thought it would be a little fling, over with before it began. I swear to God, Nancy, I tried. I tried desperately."

Her gaze riveted on his face, her breathing came in short, quick gasps as her chest heaved rapidly.

Robert glanced at Nancy and quickly looked away.

The impact of what Robert was telling her was mind-boggling. "What does this mean?"

"Nancy, I can't tell you how sorry I am," he said, looking at her again.

"I don't want to hear how sorry you are! I want to

know what this means?"

"I'm moving out."

"You can't do that!"

"I won't take from your life any more than I already have. You can keep the apartment and everything in it."

"I don't want this apartment or the things in it! I want you. Robert, I love you. Please, what did I do wrong? I'll do anything to make us right again."

"You didn't do anything wrong. You're wonderful and I do care for you, but I love someone else. I'm the one who's wrong—I can't deny what I'm feeling."

"You love her more than me?" she asked incredulously. "Who is she? How is it that she came into our lives and stole you from me?"

"I don't know. It just happened."

"It didn't just happen. You let it happen. Who is she? Where did you meet her?

"I met her while working on the merger."

"She was in Dallas with you, wasn't she?"

"Yes."

"Ohhhhhh."

"We decided it was time to tell you the truth."

"Well, bully for the both of you! What do you want, a damn medal? How long have you known her to include her in making decisions about my life?"

"I didn't mean it that way."

"How long?"

"Since last October."

"You've been sneaking around behind my back for eight months?"

"No, not in the beginning. I swear."

"You swearing don't mean a damn thing to me. You were sleeping around behind my back!"

"We came together because of the merger. A few months ago we both realized that we were in love and we couldn't fight it anymore."

"Well you should've fought harder. I knew you were gone too much. I should have known it wasn't just business," Nancy sobbed into her hands.

"You couldn't have known. I was living a lie. I lied to you and I'm deeply sorry."

"If you're so sorry, then forget about her. So you had an affair. Men do that. I forgive you. We can get beyond this. We have three years to fall back on. Please stay with me."

"Nancy...."

"Just think about it, okay? What about our plans? The house we dreamed of in Connecticut, the family you wanted. Robert, we had lots of good times together and we can have much more. Remember the time we went to Acapulco and we went hang gliding? You said the only other feeling that took your breath away like that was when you fell in love with me."

"And I still love you, just not the way you want me to. It wouldn't be right for me to keep stringing you along, cheating on you."

"But if you give us some time, it could be the way it used to."

"Nancy, we'll always be friends."

"I don't want to be your friend!" she shrieked, glaring at him.

Robert stared down at his hands.

"I'm not good enough for you, am I?"

"That's a ridiculous thing to say. What I've done has nothing to do with you," he said.

"Of course it does. If it has nothing to do with me,

then why are we having this conversation? Why am I in pain?"

Gazing at a spot on the carpet, Robert didn't answer.

"So what is she, a Connecticut blue blood?"

"Nancy, stop this."

Nancy gasped. Looking away and covering her mouth with her hands, she cried. The sobs tore at her throat. The tears poured over her hands.

His elbows resting on his thighs still, Robert pressed his forehead to his hands, shielding the tears that eased down his cheeks.

"You finally got what you wanted, huh? A high-powered corporate attorney making the big dollars like you. Your lovemaking must be really grand, huh?"

"Don't do this."

"What's her name?" she asked, wiping her face with both hands."

"Her name is unimportant," he answered, wiping away his own tears.

"It is to me! What is her name?"

"Her name is Shenoah Wells," he said finally.

"That's not a name a blue blood would have."

Robert looked away.

"What kind of name is that?"

Looking at Nancy again, Robert held her gaze.

"Answer me! What kind of name is that?"

"Shenoah is African American," he said, looking at her intently.

"Oh God, oh God…."

"I'm sorry, Nancy, but I love her. Please try and understand," Robert said, slowly getting to his feet.

"You want me to understand that you've been sleeping with a nigger and me too! Don't ask me to understand, because I can't! I won't! How could you do this to me? How could you screw a black person? They're dogs!"

"Nancy, I'm sorry I hurt you, but I won't let you talk about her or black people like that. I plan to marry Shenoah."

"You don't mean that, Robert. You can't. We're supposed to get married."

"If I could change things, I would."

"You can. Just forget about her," she pleaded.

"I can't."

"If you have children with her, they'll be black. You don't want black children."

"I'll love them no matter what color they are."

"But they might not be black or white. You don't want children who don't know where they belong!"

"Our children will know that they belong to both of us. I'm sincerely sorry, Nancy, for hurting you."

"Stop saying you're sorry! You're not sorry or you would've thought of me before you lay down with that black slut!"

"I know you're hurting, but she is not the one you should be attacking. I'm the one at fault."

"Damn right you are! I don't understand this. You don't even like black people!"

"I never said that. I don't care what color her skin is. She's a human being just like you and me."

"That's a stupid thing to say! White people have always cared about the color of black people's skin. That's why slavery! That's why the Civil War! That's why segregation! That's why civil rights! That's why affirmative action! That's why employment and economic discrimination! That's why my life is a lie!"

"Nancy, calm down. What does your life have to do with black people?"

"Get out! Get out of here!"

"Nancy, calm down!"

Leaping up out of the chair, Nancy charged at Robert with her fists. "Get out before I kill you!"

Robert caught her wrists in his hands and held her at arms' length away from him. Unable to free herself from his iron grip, she began kicking. Robert pushed her back down into the chair and jumped back. Nancy crumpled over onto her thighs and sobbed pitifully into her hands.

"I'll get my clothes later. I'm sorry," Robert said again, before snatching his suit jacket off the back of the closet door and rushing out of the apartment, slamming the door behind him with such force that it popped open.

At the top of the stairs he ran headlong into Monica. "Excuse me," he said, grabbing Monica to keep her from falling backwards down the stairs.

Glimpsing Robert's face and seeing that he was obviously upset, she asked, "Are you all right?"

"Excuse me," he responded, looking away and trotting down the stairs.

Monica watched as he raced down the stairs and out of the building before she went to the apartment door he had come out of—Nancy Michaels' apartment. The man who had let her in downstairs on his way out, after she had rung the bell twice, had told her it was the apartment at the top of the stairs. She raised her fist to knock on the open door but, hearing the crying from within, instead slipped inside the apartment and quietly closed the door behind her.

Chapter 21

The heart-wrenching sobs echoing throughout the apartment drew Monica to Nancy's bedroom door. Oblivious to Monica's presence, Nancy lay on the bed on her stomach, her face buried in her folded arms, her body convulsing from the deep gulps of breath she took between sobs. Nancy's obvious anguish did nothing to sway Monica from her purpose.

"You should cry your damn eyeballs out, you vicious bitch. You don't get an ounce of sympathy from me."

Turning her tear-drenched face to look toward the door, Nancy stopped crying instantly. She pushed herself up on her knees and off the bed in one movement. With her hands, she quickly began wiping her face and eyes dry.

"Are those tears for the man that got away?" Monica asked sarcastically. "I saw him; good-looking man. Kind of in a hurry to get away from you, wasn't he?"

"Get the hell out of my apartment or I'll call the

police." Nancy blurted angrily, her voice hoarse from crying.

"Do call the police. I have something I'd like to tell them also. Perhaps they'll find my story more interesting than yours, if you know what I mean?"

"I don't know what you're talking about. Just get out."

"Yes you do. I notice you haven't asked me how I know where you live. Does the name Calvin James mean anything to you?" Monica challenged, stepping into the room.

Nancy's hands began to shake.

"Cat got your tongue? According to Mr. James, you had no problem talking when you plotted my abduction."

"That's a lie! I never did…."

"*Shut up!*" Monica shouted, pointing her finger at Nancy. "Don't even try it! I'm a half a second off your ass and I'll gladly tell the police that I kicked it and why."

"Don't threaten me. I'm not afraid of you," Nancy responded, backing up as Monica came closer.

"Oh no? The information I have says that you ought to be. Wouldn't the DA love to hear that one of his assistants plotted to abduct an opposing attorney, who happens to be her cousin? Must be really fulfilling to have a sideline as a criminal—a criminal who, by the way, changed her name in order to hide her true identity as a woman of color, albeit the color is infinitesimal. What the hell did you think you were doing?"

"Get out of my apartment! You want to tell on me? You go ahead. I don't give a damn. Just get away from me!" Nancy shrieked, starting to walk past Monica.

"Oh no you don't. Not this time." Monica said, grabbing Nancy by the arm.

"Get your hands off me!"

"Gladly," Monica said, shoving Nancy onto the bed onto her back.

"Oh! I'll…."

"Don't even think about it. Because if you put your hands on me this time, I will lay your ass out."

Regaining her balance, Nancy leaped to her feet in front of Monica and drew back her fist.

Standing solidly with both her fists raised to her chest, Monica said threateningly between clenched teeth, "Try me."

Neither one moved.

Nancy's eyes were drawn to the vein that visibly pulsed at Monica's right temple. She knew that Monica's rage was real and dangerous. The very things that she had feared had happened—she had lost Robert, and now she could lose her career and her freedom.

Monica read the weakening of Nancy's challenge in her eyes and ordered, "Back off!"

Lowering her arm, Nancy turned and flopped down on the bed, turning toward the window away from Monica, who dropped her fists and stood looking down at her.

"Why? I just want to know why you would do something as vile as that? That was my life you were messing with."

Nancy continued looking out the window, though she saw nothing but one lone lit light bulb across the way on the back of a building.

"Don't just sit there; answer me," Monica demanded.

"I don't know!"

"Yes the hell you do."

"You wanna know?" Nancy asked belligerently, turning to face Monica. "I did it to keep you from destroying my life."

"You stupid bitch. How was I going to destroy your life, tell your little secret? Don't flatter yourself. You were never that important to me. I never had any intentions of exposing you. Yet, because you thought I would, you sent two thugs after me. I could kill you just thinking about that night," Monica said, jabbing her finger at Nancy. "At the very least, I should go to your boss."

"Why don't you?"

"Hey. Don't think I won't. You're not saying anything tough. You know as well as I do, the very career and life-style you've tried to protect will cease to exist immediately once it's known what you've done and why. And, if I'm not wrong, one of the things you were protecting, your love life, was what I met running out of the building on my way in. What happened? Did he find out that your blood wasn't lily-white?"

"I don't have to take this crap from you. Whatever you're going to do, do. Just get the hell out of my life!"

"You'll take whatever I tell your ass to take and like it. I have a few things to say to you and I'm going to say them."

"Well, I'm not going to be your captive audience," Nancy said, jumping to her feet and sprinting for the bedroom door.

Monica beat her to the door and, slamming it shut, said, "Think again. You are a captive audience of one. You get your narrow ass into that chair over there before I kick it over there."

"You touch me and I'll make enough noise to bring my neighbors running."

"Go ahead. We'll see how neighborly they'll be when

I say who I am and what you tried to do to me. In fact, why don't we talk even louder so they can hear us."

Again they faced off and again Nancy backed down. Stomping angrily over to the window looking out over the backyard, she folded her arms across her chest and stared out at the single light across the way.

Monica stayed at the door.

"I despise you," Nancy said bitterly.

"Believe me, the feeling's mutual. Right now I hate you even more for making me feel so enraged. A few weeks ago I wanted to tell you that I regretted our childhood conflicts, but every time I approached you, you slapped me in the face with your nasty mouth. I saw immediately that you didn't want me around for fear that I might let it slip that you were not Nancy Michaels after all but little Miss DeeAnn Taylor. I told myself, 'that's all right, it's her life, her choice to live it as she chooses.'" Monica kept her eyes on Nancy while hanging her pocketbook on the doorknob behind her. "You know, I didn't have to be up in your face. We weren't friends as kids; I surely wasn't expecting to become your bosom buddy at this late date. Other than in that courtroom, as far as I was concerned, I didn't know you. But then I find out that you paid someone to get rid of me, maybe even to kill me."

"Killing you was never part it."

"Right. You can say that now, but you're not completely stupid. You know damn well that anything could have happened. What were they supposed to do? Grab me, coddle me and then bring me home and tuck me in?" she asked, stepping away from the door. "If they had succeeded, were you going to appear in court the next day as cool as a cucumber, unfeeling, uncaring

204

about what you had done to me?"

"If you must know, I regret what I did. I'm not proud of it," Nancy said, still looking out into the night but sneaking a look at Monica's reflection in the window pane.

"That's of no comfort to me. It never should have been a germ of an idea in your head. What did I ever do to you to make you put my life in danger? How could you hate me so much?"

Turning and glaring at Monica, Nancy sneered, "I've always hated you. I've always hated the way you looked at me and made me feel like I didn't belong in your family; the way you teased me and called me a half breed; you and your friends talking about me and snickering and giggling whenever you saw me. I hated the private jokes you and your brother shared whenever I was in the same room. I hated to leave the house because of you."

"Don't put that crap or any of that other bull on me," Monica said, shaking her hand at Nancy. "You're the one who looked down on us. Like you were better because you looked white. Damn right I had something to say about you and your nasty attitude."

"No, you had something to say because your big mouth was always open. You're the one who thought you were better because you were pure black."

"You sound stupid."

"You're the one who's stupid."

"Not as stupid as you. It had nothing to do with color. You spoiled every family gathering because you were always pouting or acting stuck-up. I remember one Christmas you rolled your eyes at me and I pulled your hair. You cried like I'd scalped you. No one wanted to hear why I pulled your hair. Grandma DeeDee pinched me, scolded me. But you, you were rocked on her lap like a big baby."

"Jealous that you weren't on her lap?"

"Not one bit. Especially when I saw how you sat stiffly perched on her lap, your face a mask of disgust. You didn't like your own grandmother any better than anyone else because she was black too. Perhaps it's fortunate she didn't seem to notice that you didn't like her touching, much less coddling you."

"So what? Was I supposed to let everybody touch me because they were family and felt like it? I hated people pawing on me, touching my hair. 'You're so pretty, your hair's so pretty,'" Nancy sneered, shivering at the thought.

"You're a cold-hearted bitch."

"So are you."

"Are you going to tit-for-tat me to death? Was being touched lovingly by your grandmother so bad? Many a time I wanted to grab you and shake you until your brain kicked in and sent messages to your heart to thaw out. I saw how your parents agonized over trying to please you, trying to get you to like them, while you didn't give a damn about them."

"That's none of your goddamn business," Nancy shrieked, pointing her finger at Monica, her chest heaving.

"Yes the hell it is," Monica responded, stepping away from the door, her hands on her hips. "It became my business when I saw my uncle upset and angry because his precious daughter gave him her ass to kiss. He's my family too. But then, you don't understand the concept of family, do you? If you did, you wouldn't have turned your back on your mother, father, or brother, and you certainly would not have attempted to harm me. You were a stuck-up spoiled brat who didn't deserve the attention you got or the family you got."

"I didn't choose the family I got. I didn't want the family I got. Wendy and Douglas had no right to condemn me to a life of shame and rejection. I'm living a lie because of their lust."

"Shame?" Monica asked incredulously, her arms flopping to her sides. "Girl, your parents love each other and your birth was part of that love."

"Who are you to talk? Are you mixed race? No. You're not the child of two people who come of people who hate each other. People so different ethnically and culturally should never come together and have children. They force their children to deal with the confusion of having to choose one race over the other or straddle the fence and say they're both to keep from offending either parent. The children are guiltless, yet the prejudices of society make them the victims. You don't have to contend with these same two races of people who hate you for their own reasons. If they knew, white people would hate me for having a drop of black blood in my veins, and black people would hate me because I have too much white blood."

"That's an excuse, a cop-out. Sure, black people have discriminated among themselves, but the light-skinned blacks have always been accepted by the darkest of blacks. That can't always be said of light-skinned blacks accepting dark-skinned blacks. That color brainwashing goes deep. Of course there are still plenty of white people who have a problem accepting an interracial couple and their mixed offspring, but even they would accept

207

the likes of you before me with my brown skin."

"One of the things I've always hated about you," Nancy said, pointing her finger at Monica, "is that you thought you knew everything. How can you presume to speak for me? Until you've been in my skin, you should keep your damn mouth shut. As far back as I can remember, I've heard blacks call light-skinned blacks 'yalla,' 'red bone,' 'half-breed,' 'wannabes,' and 'mullato.' Those were black kids in school taunting me, not white kids. And I'm sure you've met your fair share of white people who think that black and mixed-race people are revolting. I hear them talk when there are no blacks around. Even if no one ever guessed that I was mixed, how do you think I feel inside? Did you ever have to ask yourself, who am I?"

"No, I never have, but if you asked yourself that, then you should have come up with more than white."

"Don't tell me what I should be! As a child I said I was white. How could I say that I was black when I looked white?"

"No, you wouldn't want to do that," Monica said, wanting to sit down but not doing it. "Interestingly, I see you didn't have a problem denying your father and his people. What about your mother's people?"

"Leave my mother's family out of this."

"Why? Because they love you so? Accept it, they disowned her and you."

"You don't know that. If Wendy had taken me to them, they would have accepted me."

"Dream on. Girl, you better wake up. Your puritanical white grandparents were always a stone's throw away in Lansing. They didn't care if you exhaled carbon dioxide or gold dust; you were just not white enough for them."

"Shut up!" Nancy snapped.

"Face it. In thirty years they have never opened their arms to you, but your black family has and you spit on us. I'm proof of that," she said, pretending to wipe her chin.

Nancy looked away.

"Now that I think of it, why didn't you take the middle road and say you were Hispanic or Brazilian? That way, you wouldn't have to hide the black members of your family."

"You're a bitch."

"That's real brilliant."

"Get out," Nancy said, pointing at the door, her anger so intense she thought she might choke.

"In time," Monica said matter-of-factly. "Still, I find it interesting that you chose to live in Park Slope, which probably has more interracial marriages and mixed-race children per square block than any other community in New York City. I bet you feel real comfortable over here, don't you? Except they don't know that you're one of them, do they?"

"Screw you! I'll live wherever I feel like living."

"Except among blacks. But you should look at your neighbors and a whole lot of interracial families. These people love each other. Their colors cease to exist when they become families. Obviously, love is more powerful than color or race. You know, it just dawned on me what your problem is."

"My problem is you."

"I buy that. But I think the real problem is that you think you're the first person in America with white and black blood in your veins. I think you had better step back in time to maybe the sixteen hundreds when the first slaves were brought to this country. Sorry, dear, you're not the first and you definitely won't be the last mixed-race child born on this earth."

"I know that!"

"You don't act like you know. I'd bet my life that there are those who made similar choices like you, but I'm also sure there are thousands more who are equally proud of their black and white ancestry. The difference with you is that you've hurt your black father and your white mother. You don't love either one."

"Don't tell me how I feel about my mother!" Nancy yelled, drawing her fists up to her chest. Tears were threatening, but she wouldn't let Monica think that she'd won. "You don't know how I feel about my mother."

"I don't? I guess you love her, right? Then why hasn't she seen you in years?"

"I write her."

"Oh, please. You don't mean those sterile Christmas cards you send out every year? By the way, you didn't fool her or your father with that business about calling from a phone booth on his poker nights; he knew you were avoiding him. And giving your mother a post office box number was real loving. Did you think they'd turn up on your doorstep?"

"I want you out of here," Nancy said weakly. She was bone tired, and this conversation was draining the last ounce of strength she had left after being slapped with Robert's betrayal. She hated that Monica knew about what she had done, but it was all too true. She had told Wendy that mailboxes were constantly broken into in New York City. For the past three years, she had not called home and she had slackened up on sending the Christmas cards. Her fear that they would want to visit her was ever present when she had left home. But that fear was unfounded; after all, no one had known that she had changed her name.

"I bet you do. Did you ever consider the fact that your father has to be an exceptional man if your mother was willing to lose so much to be with him?"

"Where was this love of my mother's life, who called himself my father, my guardian, my protector, when I was raped by his friend?" The words spilling out of Nancy's mouth surprised even her.

Chapter 22

"Raped? When? Who raped you?"

"You tell me what kind of father hands his child over to be raped and then thanks the man for his sordid deed?"

"Are you crazy? Uncle Douglas never did such a thing," Monica said, waving her hand at Nancy.

"Don't tell me what I know to be fact!" she screamed. "I was the one raped, not you! I was the one violated by the son of a bitch who forced himself inside my young body to satisfy his filthy, disgusting lust. I cried for my father to come and save me from the pain of that assault, but he...."

"Wait a minute," Monica said, putting up both her hands to stop Nancy from talking. "When did this happen? You can't believe that your father condoned your rape."

"I do and he did! He left me with the bastard."

"DeeAnn...."

"That's not my name!"

"Pardon me. Nancy. You can't tell me that your father knew about what happened to you. If he had known, he would have killed the bastard. I don't think he knows about you being raped to this day. I've never heard anything about such a thing. My mother would have surely known if your father knew."

"Forget it," Nancy said solemnly, realizing that she had spoken for the first time in her life about what she had always thought of as a recurring childhood nightmare. She had always felt that to talk about it meant that it was possibly true, and therefore she had remained silent. Her face grew hot, her legs trembled. Seeing Monica seemed to unlock the memories so long ago buried, especially at night when she couldn't sleep. Now she knew it was a memory and not a dream.

"No, let's not forget it," Monica said, her intense feelings of anger beginning to subside slightly. "How old were you?"

"None of your business. I want you out of here."

"What else is new? But I think I'll stay just the same."

Nancy glared briefly at Monica. Talking to Monica at all was strange, but talking to her about something as personal as a rape was stranger still. While she didn't want to talk, she could not deny the sense of relief she was feeling.

Staring back at Nancy, Monica stood with her arms folded at her waist. This revelation was not what she expected to hear, nor was she prepared for the sadness she felt.

Nancy turned again to the window, away from Monica's softening stare. The light across the way seem to shoot rays of light out from the bulb. Like one lone bright star in the sky, it drew the eye and held it. Finally, resting her forehead against the pane, she said, "I think I was six years old."

"My God! What do you remember?"

Exhaling deeply, she said, "I remember after he hurt me, he said, 'Stop crying for your daddy. He said it was okay for me to do this to you.'"

"That was a lie."

"I don't know that."

"Yes, you do. Your father has anguished for years over why you don't love him, why you don't talk to him. If he knew, would he have to wonder?"

Nancy didn't know what to answer.

"Don't you realize that you were told a lie? A six-year-old child can be told almost anything and that child will believe it. Did he also tell you not to tell?"

"Yes," Nancy said dejectedly, sitting down in the chair near the window. She glanced over at Robert's picture on her nightstand. Robert had, without a doubt, betrayed her. But if what Monica was saying was true, and the hatred for Douglas she had lived with all of her life was because of the rape, then her pain was greater because of the loss of her family. Was it possible that he really did not know?

"Right there is your truth," Monica said, sitting down at the foot of the bed. "If your father knew about it, then telling him would not have been a problem. Have you gone all these years with that pain hidden away in your memory believing that your father betrayed you?"

Again she glanced over at Robert's picture.

"In the beginning I was too afraid to tell; he said he would come back and do it again and hurt me worse. Then I tried to forget about it, but every now and then I would dream about it until I actually thought it was a

214

nightmare. It's only today, this moment, that I realize that it actually happened. But," she said, clutching her head, "I always felt that there was something hidden away in my mind, something I was supposed to know about. It was like it was there but I couldn't pull it out."

"Do you remember who the man was? Was he someone who was around all the time?"

"No, he was only at our house that one time that I know of. As best I can remember, he was visiting Douglas while Wendy was at work. He must've come over after I went to sleep because he wasn't there before I went to bed."

"Do you know where your father was?"

"I realized later that Douglas had gone to pick up Wendy. He apparently asked this man to stay with me and Winston," Nancy said reflectively, tears brimming and spilling down her cheeks. She hugged her body tightly. "I awakened because of the pain in between my legs. My legs were pulled wide apart. I felt like my lower body was up off the bed. The top of my head was pressed into the mattress. I couldn't close my legs. I couldn't understand why I couldn't close my legs. Down there, he was jabbing me with something hard. It hurt. I screamed, and a big hand covered my mouth. Out of the darkness, a voice whispered, 'I'll split you like a chicken if you scream again.'"

"Was he a black man?" Monica asked carefully, almost afraid of the answer.

Nancy slowly shook her head. Closing her eyes briefly, tears poured from under her lids. "I really don't know," she said finally. "I can't say without question whether the man was black or white. The room was dark. My bedroom door was usually left ajar so that light from the hall would stream in so it wouldn't be so dark. I could not see anything but blackness. I could hear nothing but breathing. It almost seemed unreal, except I was in pain. A big strong force I could not see held me in its grip."

"You must've been scared to death."

"I didn't think the pain would ever go away. Before he left the room, he told me to go back to sleep. I didn't. I lay in my bed withering in pain, staring into the darkness above me. To this day, I won't sleep in a dark room."

Speaking softly, Monica asked, "Were you still awake when your parents came home?"

Nancy glanced over at Monica and then quickly lowered her eyes. "When Wendy and Douglas returned, I could hear Douglas outside my room saying, 'Thanks for taking care of my babies.' To me, that confirmed what the man had said."

"That bastard. I wish we could castrate the molesters of children."

"If only we could," Nancy agreed, feeling an inner calm she had never known before.

"Your mother didn't notice anything when she bathed you the next day?"

Trying to remember the days that followed the rape, Nancy didn't answer right away.

"I don't recall her saying anything about it, though I know I was in pain for a long time."

"He must not have been a well-endowed or normal size man or he would have split you and drawn blood. Your mother would have noticed that," Monica surmised. "DeeAnn, is that why you've hated your father all these years?"

At this moment, she felt more like DeeAnn than Nancy and did not correct Monica. She looked down at her hands and said, "I honestly believed that Douglas had left the house so that this man could hurt me. I blamed him for that pain. I blamed him for allowing someone to hurt me."

"Apparently that belief set the pattern for your relationship with him."

"I never understood why I hated him so. I always thought it was because he was black. But knowing now that the rape was real explains why I reacted as I did when I caught him and Wendy having sex."

"When was this?"

"It must've been soon after the rape. I was still very young. One night when I was supposed to be asleep, in the quiet of the night, I heard Douglas grunting. Wendy was moaning just as loudly. I got out of bed and tiptoed to their bedroom door, which was open. The head of their bed was next to the door and, in the dimly lit room, I saw Douglas' contorted, sweaty black face above Wendy. I had never seen his face screwed up like that before. He was on top of Wendy; her legs were spread out to the sides around him. To me, it looked like Douglas was holding her down against her will. He was slamming his body against hers. He looked like he was hurting her. Wendy's face was flushed and screwed up too. I screamed, startling them both. Douglas jumped off of Wendy, but he was tangled up in the sheets, and he fell headfirst off the bed onto the floor. I cried for some time before Wendy could calm me down. As for Douglas, I wouldn't talk to him and I wouldn't let him touch me from that day on."

"And he never knew why."

Nancy sobbed softly into her hands, "I know now that they were making love."

Monica felt her own throat tighten. She pressed her lips together to keep from crying. Still, the tears welled up in her eyes.

"Have you been happy at all?"

Without uncovering her face, Nancy asked tearfully, "How could I? Without even remembering the rape exactly, I never knew who I was supposed to be happy as, DeeAnn or Nancy."

"Is that why you cried so when I told you once that, even under that top layer of white skin, you were black?"

"I cried because I realized that you and anyone who knew me as DeeAnn would know that and keep me from being who I was supposed to be."

"And you were supposed to be Nancy?"

She hesitated before answering. "When I was in the third grade, there was a pretty white girl I thought I looked like, except she had blonde hair. Her name was Nancy. When I saw her the first day of school, I thought, that's who I'm supposed to be, not DeeAnn Taylor. Alone in my room in front of the mirror, I became Nancy."

"No one ever knew?"

"Wendy did. I asked her to call me Nancy, but she said Grandma DeeDee would be hurt because I was named after her. I left it alone."

"Did she know how you felt about being mixed-race? I mean, did you ever tell her that you were confused or didn't understand who you were?"

"Now how was I, a small child, going to put into words my confusion about race and color; when grown-ups, scholars, black and white, hadn't been able to clear up those issues for themselves?"

Looking forlornly at Robert's picture, Nancy continued talking. She didn't think she could stop talking. "I remember when Winston was born. I was five. I could see that his skin color was different from mine. I thought there was mud on him. I even asked Wendy to wash the dirt off of him."

Monica shook her head sadly.

"She laughed and said his skin wasn't dirty, that he got his coloring from Douglas and I got mine from her. This was supposed to be a good thing that each of us resembled one of them. It was when she explained that Winston and I were black, but really mixed race, black and white, that I was confused."

"Any child would be."

"What I couldn't understand was why I couldn't be white when I looked white. I could understand Winston being black; he looked black. I didn't know anything about societal race pigeonholing. I figured if we were called black because of Douglas, then why couldn't we, me in particular, be called white because of Wendy?"

"Because of slavery and the purity of the white race," Monica said flatly, crossing her legs.

"Yes, but how was I to understand that, looking the way I did? At this point in my life, it goes beyond looks. The calendar year might be 1990 and not 1790, but conditions and attitudes have not changed so much for black people in America that the white man is willing to step aside and say, 'Hey brother, it's your turn to run things,'" Nancy said, thinking that if she could explain her reasons for living her life as she had, it would make sense to Monica. But it didn't make sense that she felt the need to explain herself at all.

"I agree, the white man will never give up his scepter."

"No, he won't. This country is still run by whites, the wealth is still owned by whites, and blacks still get only what whites want them to have, and that's not very much. The handful of Reginald Lewises, Oprah Winfreys, Bill Cosbys, and Michael Jacksons are more the exception than the norm. I figured if my life could be easier because of my white skin, then I would cash in on it. We live in a society that says that whites are the beautiful ones, the powerful ones, and I was able to cross the line into that world unnoticed."

"But at what price? You're literally alone," Monica said, looking earnestly into Nancy's water-filled eyes.

Biting on her lower lip, Nancy turned away from Monica just as fresh tears rolled down her cheeks. Being alone without family or friends had been her life for so long that she had known no other way of living until Robert. She squeezed her eyes shut to still the tears. Hugging herself tightly around the waist, she tried also to still the ache in her stomach.

"Are you all right?" Monica asked, wanting to go over to her. She didn't know that she could feel the pain of another person so intensely.

Nancy opened her eyes and a flood of tears rushed down her cheeks. "Did you know that my birth certificate gives my race as white?"

"No."

"Well, it does. Wendy didn't discover it for weeks after I was born. The hospital saw a white woman who gave birth to a white looking baby. She said she left it because it really didn't matter. I used to wonder how she felt about her two children looking so differently."

"You should have asked her."

220

"I couldn't. But this is why I vowed never to have children. I was too afraid that they wouldn't come out looking like me. No, I've never known true happiness. To know that, I would have had to be confident in who I was. And I wasn't. I was always afraid that someone would find out that I was living a lie. I was afraid to confide in anyone. I was always afraid that Robert would sense that I was hiding something."

"I noticed that you keep looking over at that picture. He's Robert, right? The guy who left here earlier?"

"I won't talk about him."

"That's all right. But I wish we'd all known about the rape."

"Would it have made a difference?"

"Of course it would have. It explains so much," Monica said, getting up and walking over to the window. She looked once at the light across the way before she turned and sat down on the window sill just behind Nancy.

Monica's closeness didn't unnerve Nancy or make her feel uncomfortable.

"Perhaps you never would have felt that way about your father. If your father had known and you had seen him beat that guy, he would have been your hero instead of your object of scorn. His color or race probably would've never bothered you. Somehow or other, it seems to me that you associated that dark room and your father's supposed betrayal with black people. I could be wrong, but it seems that way to me. It's possible that you might have felt differently about me too. I admit I was cruel to you and wanted to hurt you at every turn, but at the same time, I wanted to be friends and didn't know how to begin. I took your sour demeanor and standoffishness as a snub. I reacted in kind."

Pulling the tail of her expensive cotton blouse out of her skirt, Nancy wiped her face dry. Without looking back at Monica, she said, "I hated you because you didn't include me in your circle of friends. I envied you your friendships and the fearless way you approached life. You always looked like you were having fun. I was jealous of that."

"In truth, I was jealous of you too."

Opening her eyes wide at this revelation, Nancy looked back over her right shoulder at Monica and asked, "What for?"

Smiling weakly at the memory, Monica answered, "I used to wish that I had long hair like yours."

"Really?"

"Yes. Every time I saw you flip your hair out of your face, I'd want to snatch you bald," she said, chuckling. "I wanted long hair too, but my hair just wouldn't grow like that. My mother had a time trying to convince me that my hair was nice and that heredity and genes had something to do with hair growth. Black people grew natural curls, she said, nature's gift from hair rollers. I didn't get over the long hair blues until I was about thirteen and started wearing an afro. And when I saw that white people were trying to wear Afros too, I was cured."

"I can't say that I ever wanted an Afro; what I wanted most was friends. My childhood was anything but memorable."

"Look, we have to own up to our childhood and get beyond it. Who's to say that you would have made the same choices if the rape had not happened to you. If anything, I know that your relationship with your father would have been different."

"He probably hates me," Nancy said, tears emptying rapidly from her tired eyes.

"I don't think so. My mother says that he doesn't talk about you but that he visibly saddens at the mention of your name."

Nancy covered her face with her hands again and cried. The shame of what she had done to her family overwhelmed her.

Wiping tears away from her own eyes, Monica watched DeeAnn cry and wondered if it was too late for her to turn her life around.

After a moment Nancy lowered her hands and asked, "What am I supposed to do? I've lost Robert; I might lose my job; my life is a mess, and I don't know how to put it back together again. And if I'm ever given another chance, I don't know if I can get it right this time either."

"DeeAnn, I don't have all the answers, and all the answers are not going to come overnight. But considering what you tried to do to me and the way in which you lived your life, I think in order to heal that hurt child within and get your life back on track, whatever track that might be, you might consider going back home and making your peace with your father first. He might be the only person who can truly help you, but you have to be willing. It just might be the hardest thing you'll ever have to do, but it's a beginning."

"I don't know if I can go back."

"Yes, you can. I'll go with you."

MAMA SOLVES A MURDER

When Simone's former college roommate is arrested for murder, it appears to be an open-and-shut case, but her boss, Atlanta attorney Sidney Jacoby,

takes on the defense and assigns Simone to investigate. This is the kind of case that's right up Mama's alley, so Simone invites her for a visit. Mama's nickname is "Candi" because of her candied sweet potato complexion. She is charming, ingratiating, intuitive, and shrewd; she is also nosy, manipulative, foolhardy, and sometimes absolutely infuriating—but she has a talent for cooking and for solving mysteries.